PUSHING UP DAISIES

COURTNEY MCFARLIN

Chapter One

The short walk from my office in the resort to my cabin was an easy commute, but on days like this, I slowed down, savoring the warmth on my skin from the sun and the incredible smells of Spring in Colorado. The long winter had finally let go of its stranglehold on our tiny mountain town and I was definitely here for it.

I'd always appreciated this season, but this year, it felt special. I'd finally settled into my new job at the Valewood resort, and despite a few terrible events early on, things had quieted down. Well, at least in some ways. In other ways, my life was louder than ever. I took a deep breath before I pushed open the door of my cabin.

A chorus of tiny meows bounced around the wooden walls as three kittens scampered towards me. I'd taken in their mother, Luna, and her litter almost two months before, during a brutal snowstorm. The clowder they belonged to lived in the nearby forest, but I'd convinced Luna to stay in the cabin until the kits were older. It might be Spring, but the nights still were too cold for tiny kittens.

Jasper, the former leader of the clowder, sat on my bed. His whiskers quirked into a smile as he watched the little ruffians try out their mountaineering skills by clambering up my legs. I'd attempted to keep them corralled in a playpen while I was gone, but apparently, they'd learned how to scale the sides.

Jasper nodded proudly.

"They've grown quite strong. You've done well with them, Luna."

The white cat dipped her head and shifted her position on the chair in the corner.

"Thank you, Jasper. I'm glad you think so. A lot of the credit goes to Eden, though. Without her help, they wouldn't have made it this far."

That's me. Eden Brooks. And in case you're wondering, yes, I can understand cats. It was an ability I discovered shortly after I got a job at the resort a few months ago. My friend, Hannah Murphy, had asked me to look after the clowder when she helped me get this job, and somehow, she shared the same ability. I didn't ask too many questions about it. I worried it might suddenly disappear, which was devastating to think about. I shook off that gloomy thought and focused on the three ragamuffins who were halfway up my legs.

"Ouch, little ones. Your claws are getting very sharp."

The black kitten on my knee blinked his beautiful blue eyes at me. He was a carbon copy of his father, Oscar, a big brute of a cat who'd stayed with the clowder. He still hunted for Luna, bringing her many rodent-y treats, much to my consternation, but he refused to stay inside my cabin for long. The little girl kitten was snow white, just like her mother, but she had her father's piercing blue eyes. The third kitten, another boy, was a gray tabby, with green eyes like his mother.

I carefully picked each one up and cuddled them close before returning them to the playpen. The little girl let out a piercing meow that was startling in the small cabin. Luna leapt down and joined the kits in the playpen, distracting them. She'd begun weaning them, but I noticed she still kept the girl kitten close, paying her extra attention. I sat next to Jasper and scratched behind his ears as he purred loudly.

"When are they coming?"

I wasn't sure how old Jasper was, but the senior cat had nearly been on his last legs when I'd discovered him underneath a bush near where we fed the clowder. I'd taken him into the vet and nursed him back to health. Thankfully, he'd opted to stay with me instead of returning to the wild.

"Hannah texted a few hours ago. They're just leaving Golden Hills now, so they should be here in about a half an hour."

"Good. I'm looking forward to seeing them again. Especially Gus. He's a solid cat."

Hannah was coming for a much-anticipated visit, and bringing her delightful menagerie of cats along for the trip, and, of course, her boyfriend, Ben. Her cats, Razzy, Rudy, and Ben's cat, Gus, had been to the resort for the wedding of a friend, and had met the clowder during their investigation of a murder. I'd met them at the place I used to work, Ken Brockman's estate in southern Colorado. In a way, they were the glue that held all our threads together.

"Gus is a handsome cat," Luna said, and I noticed her whiskers had a mischievous tilt to them. "I'm looking forward to their visit as well. I bet Rudy has grown up to be quite a looker, too."

I coughed, uncomfortably shifting on the bed, while Jasper looked on with a knowing glint in his eyes. Razzy hadn't appreciated Luna's overtures to Gus when they'd visited the last time, and if her silence every time Luna's name was brought up was any sign, she hadn't forgiven the cat.

A knock at the door broke me out of my thoughts and I scurried over, opening the door to reveal my best friend, Charlie Turner. She worked the night shift at the front desk. Her brown hair was up in a ponytail, revealing the bright blue dye on the underside of her hair. She'd switched from her signature magenta color and wasn't sure if she liked it yet.

"Got room for us?" she asked as she shifted the bundle in her arms.

I smiled at the tuxedo cat in her arms.

"Hi, Benny! You sound a lot better."

Charlie had adopted Benny when we'd discovered him on the fringes of the clowder, desperately sick with a respiratory illness. He wasn't the friendliest cat, but he adored my friend, and had adapted to living with her. Thanks to her care, he no longer wheezed every time he took a breath. He'd been given a clean bill of health from our local vet, which meant he could visit the kittens. I'd been surprised the grumpy cat enjoyed their company, but they adored him. The loud chorus of meows from the playpen started up as soon as they spotted him.

Benny said nothing to me, which wasn't unusual. But he didn't hiss like he usually did, which I took as a sign he was thawing. Charlie put him down and he stalked over to the playpen, twitching his tail as the kits began scaling the walls. She walked over to say hi to Jasper before plopping down on the floor next to the playpen. The kittens abandoned Benny to crawl over Charlie.

"Do you think Hannah will be here in time for dinner? I've heard the kitchen has something special planned."

As part of our employment package, we got to live on site at the resort, and our meals were provided for free at the dining hall. It was a benefit I'd quickly come to appreciate, especially since the food was amazing. Our boss, James Marsburg, the owner of the resort, had offered to let my friends stay in the neighboring cabin for free, meals included.

"I hope so. They're planning on it. I can't wait for you to meet her."

"Trevor said they were super cool people. Is Ethan planning on stopping out to say hello to them?"

I stilled at the mention of Ethan. We'd been thrown together a few times, thanks to three different murders that he investigated, but I hadn't seen him lately. I'd been busy focusing on learning the ropes for public relations and my schoolwork, and he'd been busy with his job as a detective. We had a connection, there was no doubt about that, but it seemed like we would be two ships crossing in the night.

"Maybe. I'm not sure. I'd rather focus on the wildflower safari. I hope everything goes without a hitch."

"Hmm. Nice change of subject. But I know it's going to be great. My best friend's the one who organized it. She's been working super hard on it."

She gave me a gentle elbow to the ribs, and I grinned. She

wasn't wrong. I'd poured my heart and soul into my work lately, and Mr. Marsburg had given me free rein to come up with ideas to promote the resort. The wildflower safari idea had come to me in a flash when I was reading about things to do in the area.

"Well, I appreciate it. I'm gonna need the support. What if no one likes it? People are booking weekend stays here just to take part in it. I drove out last weekend to double check the meadows we're going to visit and the flowers are blooming, but what if a storm sweeps through tonight and destroys them all? Ugh."

That earned me another elbow in the side, this time a little sharper, and Charlie rolled her eyes.

"Oh, Eden. There's nothing forecasted and those flowers are tougher than you think. It's right there in the name, isn't it? Wild? People are going to love it. Heck, I've lived nearby my whole life and never did something like that," she said, holding up a finger as I tried to interrupt. "And I'm not just saying that. Everything is going to be fine. You've got the guide all lined up?"

"Yep. Her name's Tessa. Her company's called Wild Peak Expeditions. She seems very capable and knowledgeable. She's going to meet us at the site. I can't believe Mr. Marsburg found us a bus to rent and everything. He's been so supportive of this idea."

"Because it's a great one! So, quit worrying."

The girl kitten picked that moment to run up my leg, yowling as loud as her tiny lungs would allow. I picked her up and cradled her in my arms while she looked at me with her wide blue eyes. So far, the kittens hadn't talked, and I wasn't sure when they would. Jasper and Luna weren't sure either, but I had a feeling this little one was going to have the voice of an opera singer when she spoke. I gave her a kiss on the forehead and put her down on the bed next to Jasper.

"Come here, kiddo," Jasper said, rolling on his side. "Talk to Uncle Jasper."

Charlie watched me for a moment and shook her head.

"They're just so stinking cute. Oh, look at that!"

I turned in time to see the gray tabby kitten spring onto Benny's back. I winced, expecting a hiss, but Benny merely shrugged his shoulders, sending the kitten into a gentle tumble down his side, before repeating the process. He might not be a fan of humans, well, at least of me, but he tolerated the babies. Luna gave an indulgent smile and settled back down on her favorite chair, curling her tail over her nose.

"Benny, do you want to stay with the kittens while we have supper?" Charlie asked.

She couldn't understand them like I could, but ever since she'd found out that I could talk to cats, she'd been talking to Benny just like he was a human. It appeared they'd worked out their own system of communication. He gave her a slow blink and turned back in time to catch the second kitten who'd launched himself at Benny's back.

"That looked like a yes to me," she said with a giggle. "At least with their uncles around, Luna can take a nap."

Between Jasper and Benny, the kits had plenty of willing babysitters, but I couldn't help but wish Oscar would spend more time with them. He seemed proud of them, but he refused to spend any more time than necessary in the cabin. My phone buzzed, and I grabbed for it.

"Uh oh," I said as I read the text. "Wendy's swamped and needs some help. I guess two safari guests showed up and they're not happy."

I shoved down the worry rising from my stomach and sprang up. Charlie was right behind me, checking her watch.

"I'm not supposed to start until after dinner time, but I can come in early and help. I wonder what's going on?"

I said a quick goodbye to the cats before heading back to the main resort building with Charlie. By the time we were close to the building, I was practically running. I was relying on everything going smoothly for this big weekend, and it wasn't a good sign that there was already an issue.

Chapter Two

Wendy shot me a look of gratitude as soon as I went through the sliding doors. I spotted a couple standing across the desk from her and my shoulders stiffened a little as I caught what the woman was saying.

"When I booked this trip, I was certain that a suite was included in the price. I can't believe you're telling me we have a regular room. Where is your boss? I need to speak to someone higher up who can actually do something about this."

The woman's voice rose to a pitch that was nearly painful as I hustled towards the front desk. Charlie followed right behind me.

"I'm afraid Mr. Marsburg has gone home for the day," Wendy said, her face drawn into a practiced smile. "But Eden is our public relations manager, and I'm sure she'll be able to help you."

The woman turned her sights on me. She was a little taller than me, and heavily built, with broad shoulders. Her light blonde hair was styled into a sleek bob with the edges turned under the curve of her jaw. I caught a flash of anger in her light blue eyes and tried to smile.

"What appears to be the problem?"

She slammed a brochure down on the table and pointed at it. I recognized the brochure. It was the one I'd painstakingly put together to promote the wildflower safari. I'd spent hours getting it just right, and Charlie had helped with the pictures. The woman stabbed at it with a lacquered stiletto shaped fingernail.

"Right here. It says all participants in the safari will be treated to a stay in one of our luxurious suites. Well? Why did I get a regular room? We paid good money for this weekend, didn't we, Milton?"

Her husband nodded, his round face filled with gloom. His stomach spilled over his waistband, while his shirt buttons appeared to be holding on for dear life.

"That's right, honey. You tell them."

From the dullness of his reply, I wondered if he was even listening. It seemed like a rote response, one he queued up on regular occasions. I gave her an encouraging nod.

"You're absolutely right... I'm sorry, I didn't catch your name."

"Darlene and Milton Prescott."

The doors slid open, and I turned to see Hannah and Ben walk into the lobby, their faces bright. They were carrying three bags with their precious cats. I waved and focused my attention back on the fuming Darlene, who was tapping her fingernail on the brochure again.

"Well?"

"I'm so sorry, Darlene. There must have been a mixup when you booked the room. We'll be happy to make that right for you," I said, swinging behind the desk while Wendy moved to the side. "Let me just double check your booking."

I typed in their names and waited for the system to load while Charlie looked over my shoulder. Their reservation popped up, but it was a standard one, not the special wildflower safari package I'd programmed for the event.

"Hmmm. It looks like you've got a standard booking. Did you book online?"

"No. I don't believe in all that new-fangled rigamarole. I called and talked to a woman. It was probably her," she said, aiming that sharp fingernail in Wendy's direction. "Let me guess, you got it wrong?"

I looked further and my shoulders tightened a little more when I saw who'd made the booking. Penny Langston, the head of housekeeping. She must have been manning the desk when the call came through. Penny had it in for me, and something told me it wasn't an honest mistake that she'd booked the room wrong. I shook off the bad vibes and smiled at Darlene.

"No worries. We've got one suite left and we'll change your room right now. It's already been cleaned, so you're ready to go."

Charlie and Wendy pitched in, getting their keycards ready, while Darlene continued to complain. My eye twitched slightly as I slid the keys across the desk to her.

"You're on the top floor, in our corner suite. It's our nicest one."

"Well. We'll see about that. Come on Milton. Get the bags."

"Yes, dear."

She scraped the keys off the desk with her fingernails and headed towards the elevators, head held high. Milton brought up the rear, burdened down with three heavy bags. I exchanged a quick glance with Wendy and Charlie before sighing in relief as the elevator whisked the Prescotts away.

"Wow," Hannah said, walking forward with a grin on her face. "That was interesting. How are you Eden? I love your hair!"

The last time she'd seen me, I had hair down to my waist and I'd still been struggling with trying to find the new me after a hard upbringing and a disastrous relationship with a man who turned out to be a homicidal maniac. Even though we talked on the phone regularly, seeing Hannah in person was a real treat. I swung around the desk and wrapped her in a hug.

"Oh, it's so good to see you! How was the drive? How are the cats? Oh, and how are you, Ben?"

Ben leaned his tall frame against the table and smiled, crinkling the corners of his jade green eyes. I'd forgotten how handsome he was. Hannah was a lucky woman. And Ben was a lucky man to have the irrepressible Hannah in his life. Wendy gasped a little behind us as he turned the full force of his smile onto the other women.

"Hi, I don't believe we've met," Ben said, nodding at my friends behind the desk.

I introduced everyone and peeked inside the carriers to say hi to the cats. Razzy pawed at the door of her bag while Hannah chuckled.

"I know, sweetheart. You want to greet Eden, too. Just be patient."

Charlie tossed me the keys to their cabin, and I led them outside. My run-in with the Prescotts was completely forgotten.

"Let's get you settled in your cabin and then we can head to the dining hall."

"I want to see the kittens," came a voice from one bag.

"Rudy, you'll have to be patient," Hannah said, her voice smooth. "We still need to get all our bags unloaded and get you guys set up."

"You're staying next to me, so visiting will be super easy," I said, opening the door to their cabin. "I'll help you get everything set up."

Hannah dropped off Razzy's bag on the bed, and headed back outside with me, chattering a mile a minute. It had been so long since I'd seen her and yet it felt like no time at all had passed. I hadn't known her long, but she'd become one of my dearest friends.

"This place is so beautiful," Hannah said, looking around as we walked back to the parking lot. "We had little time to appreciate it the last time we were here."

A shadow crossed over her face and Ben reached for her hand in a subconscious movement. I'd had little chance to see the two of them interacting, and already it was clear how much love they shared. Would I ever find someone like that? Someone who knew my moods so well they didn't even need to look to sense how I was feeling?

"A lot has changed since you were here," I said, after a moment. "Trevor is still here, but I think nearly everyone else is gone. Maybe Penny was here, though. She's worked here forever."

"I don't think I've met her, but maybe I've forgotten," Hannah said.

I grimaced, unable to contain myself.

"Hmm. You'd remember if you'd met her. Which car is yours?"

"Our Blazer is over there," Ben said, leading the way. "I think we brought more bags for the cats than for ourselves."

We shared a chuckle as he unlocked the doors and we began hauling stuff back to the cabin. It took two trips, but that gave us plenty of time to catch up. By the time we got back with the second load, it was clear the cats were ready to get out of their bags and stretch their legs.

Rudy shook himself after shooting out of his bag and looked around, eyes wide.

"Is this the same cabin we were in before? It looks different."

"No, bud. We were across the way," Ben said.

Gus strolled over to me and I bent down to scratch behind his ears. It had been ages since I'd seen the cats. Razzy was right behind him and she looked up at me with her luminous blue eyes melting my heart. I scooped her up for a hug as she nuzzled close.

"It's so good to see you, Eden. I've missed you. So, what's the lowdown? Any intrigue? It's been too quiet lately."

I glanced at Hannah, who was shaking her head. I knew about Razzy's abduction, but apparently, she'd bounced back, as curious as ever.

"Oh, Razzy. Sometimes quiet is a good thing."

"Not if you're a star reporter on the crime beat, Mama," she said as she wiggled for me to let her down. "We've got to stay on top of things. You know how much action Eden has up here. This is an exciting place."

"Well, I'm sorry to be the bearer of boring news," I said. "But things have quieted down since the snowmobile event. And I agree, Hannah, quiet is good."

"Tell us about the wildflower safari," Ben said as he organized the cat box and set up their things. "Hannah was talking about it on the way here. It sounds interesting."

I sat on the bed, laughing as Rudy vaulted up and sprang around, burning off the energy he'd likely built up on the long car ride. Razzy was busy investigating every nook and cranny with Gus.

"Maybe safari is overselling it a little, but I've got a hike planned through a popular valley that has loads of fresh flowers. The surrounding mountains are so majestic and it should be a great place to get some excellent photographs. Midway through the hike, we'll have a relaxing lunch at a lake, and then hike back to the bus. The guide is supposed to be great. I guess she knows all about the wildflowers around here. I'm excited."

Hannah patted my arm, beaming.

"I'm so proud of you, Eden. You've really come into your own. We can't wait to come along. It's going to be exciting."

"Huh," Rudy said before launching a pounce directly in front of Razzy, making her glare before setting her coat to rights. "I didn't think flowers were that exciting, but maybe I've been looking at it wrong. Oh! Are there any carnivorous flowers out there? Now that would be interesting."

I chuckled as I shook my head.

"No, I don't think so."

"Oh. Well, I'm sure it will be great."

"I hope so. Is everyone hungry? We can head to the dining hall."

"I wanna meet the kittens," Rudy said. "Can we go to your cabin, Eden?"

I didn't miss the way Razzy paused in her bathing routine and let out a tiny sigh. She dragged herself upright while Gus nuzzled her ear.

"Sure. I know Jasper is excited to see all of you again."

I left out mentioning Luna. They'd see her soon enough. Ben and Hannah brought out the harnesses, and the cats patiently waited for their turn. It was marvelous.

"All right, guys. Let's go!"

I led the way to my cabin and opened the door, much to Benny's dismay. He hissed and dove under the bed, while everyone stared.

"Who was that?" Rudy asked, his voice tremulous.

"Benny, it's okay," I said as I closed the door behind us. "You can come out."

A light growl issued from beneath the bed, so I decided not to push it. Jasper sat up from his spot on the bed while the kittens looked on, eyes wide at the newcomers. Gus and Rudy were large cats, even bigger than Oscar, and I could only imagine what they were thinking. Luna sprang out of the playpen and waltzed over, tail held high, to touch noses with the boys. I could hear Razzy muttering under her breath as she skirted the white cat and went to greet Jasper. Oh boy, this could get interesting.

We watched as the cats greeted each other, talking animatedly. I looked at Ben and tilted my head, realizing for the first time that he was following everyone's conversation. He noticed my look and smiled before fishing out a necklace from underneath his shirt.

"I'm not like Hannah," he said, showing me the stone on its leather thong. "You know, Anastasia, right? She gave me this and somehow, it enabled me to understand the cats."

"Wow. That's incredible. I wonder if I could get something like that for Charlie? She adopted Benny, and I know she'd love to talk with him."

Hannah and Ben exchanged a glance while Luna introduced the boys to the kittens. Razzy thumped down and joined them, and you could almost see the lines of dislike radiating from both female cats as they looked at each other.

"Razzy."

"Luna."

The moment of tension passed as the kits clambered over the walls of the playpen, yowling joyously. Gus looked a little overwhelmed as they climbed onto his back, snuffling around in his fur, and I couldn't help but giggle at his expression. The little girl kit sat in front of Rudy, her eyes wide as she blinked at him. He gently touched her nose, and she meowed loudly, making him jump.

"Wow, she's got some lungs! I thought I was loud."

Razzy spoke to each kit while Luna looked on, eyes narrow. Jasper chirped from the bed and I hustled over and bent down.

"It's not good to have two queens together, especially since they're not in the same clowder. I think that's enough for now."

I nodded, getting the point, and turned back to my friends.

"Everyone hungry? We'd better get to the dining hall before Danny clears out all the food."

Razzy stalked to the door, obviously ready to leave. Gus hurried after her, but Rudy looked torn as he patted the girl kit with his paw.

"Is it okay if I stay? It's been forever since I've been around kittens. Not since Callie was little."

Hannah looked at Luna, who'd relaxed now that Razzy was away from her kittens.

"Do you mind?"

"Not at all."

"Okay, bud. Best behavior, okay? I'll bring you back some food."

We said our goodbyes, and I gave Jasper a quick kiss on the forehead before ushering everyone to the dining hall. I'd never dined with cats before, unless you counted scarfing down a sandwich while they ate from their bowls, and I was looking forward to this novel experience.

Chapter Three

R azzy and Gus walked ahead of us on their leads, their furry heads bent together, deep in conversation. While I didn't want to eavesdrop, I couldn't help wondering what on earth they were talking about so seriously.

"When we were here before, Gus went undercover in the clowder," Hannah said, apparently reading my mind. "Luna, um, well, she got very attached to Gus. Razzy wasn't a fan of that."

"Mama!"

Razzy turned, and if a cat could blush, she would've been beet red. Hannah chuckled softly and bent down to stroke her furry little head.

"Sorry, baby girl."

"It's not my fault Luna is such a... Well, I won't say it, but I would like to. I would like to say it very much."

I bit my lip at the look on Ben's face and jumped in to help Razzy out of this embarrassing situation.

"I can't wait for you to meet everyone else. Luke, he's part of the kitchen staff, he's the one who always makes sure the cats have plenty of food. I go with him most nights to deliver it to the clowder. Would you like to go with us tonight?"

Razzy brightened and gave a sharp nod.

"Yes. I'd like that. Fig is still around, right?"

"She is."

"She's a straight shooter," Gus said, his deep voice startling me. "I'm glad she's in charge. She'll take good care of those cats."

Mollified, Razzy allowed Hannah to pick her up, and I led the way into the dining hall. Danny shouted from across the room, waving wildly.

"There they are! See, I told you they were gonna bring the cats. Pay up, Charlie!"

He held out his palm expectantly, but Charlie just rolled her eyes before waving at us. Carl and Wendy gave us friendly nods as I pointed out the long line of buffet tables.

"It's serve yourself. Oh my goodness, is that a prime rib? They really went all out!"

I hustled over to the first table and smiled at Luke, who was offloading a new vat of mashed potatoes. I glanced over at the table where Danny and Charlie were sitting and figured out that's where the first vat must have disappeared to. The two of them loved to fight over potatoes.

"Hi, Eden," Luke said, blushing as Hannah joined me. "You must be Hannah. Eden's talked so much about you."

"Well, I'm worried I'm not gonna be able to live up to the hype," Hannah said, her tone dry. "It's nice to meet you, Luke. Eden was telling us about how you keep the clowder fed. Thank you for doing that. I'd like to come along tonight, if that's okay?"

"Of course.. I see you brought two of your cats. Aren't there three?"

"Yes, but one stayed behind with the kittens. It's okay to have them in here, isn't it?"

"Of course. As long as they don't go back into the kitchens, it's fine. I'd pet them, but I'm allergic. Iris made sure we had plenty of food for everyone tonight. The clowder is going to be pretty excited."

Ben grabbed three trays and passed them out, while Razzy and Gus sniffed, their eyes nearly crossing at the combination of delicious smells. I loaded up my tray, getting a little extra to pass along to my feline roommates, and headed over to our usual table. Danny hopped up and made sure everyone had enough chairs, smiling when Razzy hopped into hers and sat at the table, just like a small, rather furry human.

"Look at these guys," he said, grinning with delight. "This is so great. How did you train them to do this?"

Hannah slid her tray onto the table and shrugged.

"They're very smart. You must be Danny. I've heard about you."

Danny hunched his shoulders and shot a glance at me.

"All good I hope?"

"I heard something about a potato-based rivalry," she said, covering her plate with a protective arm.

"I assure it was a gross exaggeration," he said, clutching his chest. "I'm wounded. Actually, if there's a rivalry, it's all Charlie's fault."

Charlie stuck out her tongue at Danny before shaking her head.

"You might think we're super immature. And you'd be right. It's so cool to meet you in person. You're practically famous around here."

Hannah blushed and focused on getting plates for Razzy and Gus, while Ben greeted everyone else. He folded his lanky form into a chair and dug in with gusto, nodding his head as he sampled the prime rib.

"This is incredible. You guys are pretty lucky to have an on-site meal service."

"Just wait until dessert," Charlie said, forking in a mouthful of feather-light mashed potatoes. "I heard Iris went all out. It's all very hush-hush, but I think it's going to be great."

"Well, I can't wait. Now, tell me all about yourselves," Hannah said after she slid two small plates in front of the cats.

I couldn't help but smile at how fastidious Razzy was as she carefully picked up her servings of meat and savored each bite. Gus was a little less careful, but they had better table manners than I did. I joined in the flow of conversation, recounting funny bits of our day-to-day lives here at the resort. By the time everyone was done,

Danny was already eyeing the dessert table avidly, rubbing his hands together.

"Oh, I think they're going to bring it out now. Charlie, what it's gonna be?"

"Hmm. I think tiramisu."

"No way. Cherry pie, all the way."

They bickered back and forth until Iris appeared, followed by Luke and a new kitchen staff worker I hadn't met yet. She'd replaced Amber, who'd tricked us all, hiding among us to help murder a former guest. I shook off those gloomy memories and focused on the present. The trays were laid down with a flourish, and Danny scraped his chair back to hustle over.

"Dang it," he said, shouting over her shoulder. "Guess we're even, Charlie."

Charlie pumped her fist and grinned, joining him at the table. The rest of us followed at a much slower pace and got our individual servings of tiramisu. I'd never had it before, but my exploratory sniff promised it was going to be amazing.

Once we were back at the table, Hannah poked around her dessert before glancing at the cats.

"Sorry, guys. There's chocolate in here. I'm afraid I can't share."

"That's okay, lady," Gus said, "I'm stuffed, anyway."

The others joined us, interrupting Razzy's answer, but her blue eyes never left Hannah's spoon as she sampled the dessert and groaned.

"Oh my, this is heaven."

I tried my first taste and had to agree. The kitchen staff had certainly outdone themselves. Once we were finished with our desserts, Charlie rushed off to man the front desk and everyone else trailed off, back to their cabins, leaving me alone with Hannah, Ben, and the cats. Luke and the staff had everything cleaned up by then, but they were still clanging around in the kitchen.

"Ready to see the clowder?"

"Yeah, let's go," Razzy said, hopping down from her chair.

Hannah groaned and shook her head as she got up and shuffled behind me.

"I ate too much, but that was incredible."

"It was. I'm so grateful you found me this job, Hannah. I don't think I can ever thank you enough. You changed my life."

She held up a finger and shook her head of curly blonde hair.

"Nope. You changed that. All I did was help you get your foot in the door. Everything else? That's all you."

A warm fuzzy feeling wrapped itself around my heart as I stopped near the door of the kitchen, waiting for Luke. Ben yawned and stretched.

"How's the new detective agency going?" I asked, realizing we'd monopolized the conversation that evening.

He flashed a smile and put an arm around Hannah.

"Great. It was slow at first, but I'm getting more clients. I've got some great co-workers, so I can't complain," he said, winking at the cats. "It's the best thing I ever did."

I bounced in place a little, tickled that everything was working out for my favorite couple. If there ever was someone who deserved nothing but the best, it was these two. Luke popped out of the kitchen door, his gangly arms laden down with two stacked trays. Ben hustled over and took the top one.

"Thanks, man. Everybody ready?"

"Lead the way," Hannah said, rushing ahead to get the door for them. "It's been a while since we were here."

We talked about the clowder cats as we walked, although it was tough not to mention the conversations I'd had with Fig. I'd told Charlie about my abilities, but that was it. No one else could know I talked with the cats, and I wasn't about to reveal Hannah's secrets either. Halfway there, Razzy tired of walking and Hannah boosted her into her arms, while Gus kept striding ahead. We reached the clearing where we usually fed the cats and I helped Luke get everything set up. One by one, they appeared, with Fig in the lead. She took her normal spot on the stump and eyed Hannah with her glowing yellow eyes.

"I remember you."

"Hi, Fig. You're looking well."

Fig sniffed and looked at Razzy in Hannah's arms.

"I see you've come back as well. Where's the third?"

"He's back with Luna's kits," Razzy said, dipping her head slightly towards the brown cat. "It's good to see you."

Gus approached while Hannah put Razzy down and the cats talked amongst themselves. Ben smiled as the smaller cats came forward to eat their fill. Fig must have said something to them, since they didn't seem hesitant around Hannah and Ben. Willow padded over and immediately took to Hannah, chattering away. Eventually, Ollie came forward, eyeing the mashed potatoes hungrily.

"Oh yeah, that gravy looks good," he said, licking his chops.

Gus nodded at the rotund tuxedo cat before turning his attention back to Fig.

"Where's Oscar? I don't see him around."

Fig shrugged before hopping down from the stump.

"He's around. He's probably trying to get into Eden's cabin. It's about time to send those kits back. They need to learn their hunting skills. I know you took them in out of kindness, Eden, but it's time they join their clowder."

She walked towards the food, settling down next to Ollie, and I exhaled loudly. I wasn't ready to see them go, and I still hadn't mentioned Luna's request to Fig. I kept meaning to, but every time it came up, I chickened out. I wasn't sure how she'd feel about the girl kitten being adopted by a human.

Hannah shot me a curious look, and I shook my head slightly. Maybe she'd know what to do. Her wisdom had guided me through many sticky moments. Luke finished up gathering the old platters we'd left behind from the day before.

"The cats are sure chatty tonight," he said, smiling shyly. "I think they were thrilled about their special treats."

If he had questions about why there was so much meowing going on, he didn't ask, and I appreciated it. Once everyone was done, we headed back to the cabins. Luke split off at the dining hall, waving his goodbyes before disappearing inside. Hannah patted her purse where she'd stashed a few leftovers for Rudy, while I had my little bundle for everyone else. We were almost at my cabin when a dark form jumped out at us, hissing like mad.

My heart almost stopped before I recognized Oscar squaring off against Gus. The big Maine Coon was growling low in his chest, towering over the black cat with the startling blue eyes. Razzy let out a yowl before stalking in between the two males, breaking apart the stand-off.

"Really? We do not act like ruffians," she said, hissing a little at the end.

Oscar straightened, and his nose worked as he sniffed at Razzy's face. Gus growled again and stood, every muscle taut. Ben and Hannah exchanged worried glances.

"It's been a while, queen," Oscar said, his tone rich. "You are still as beautiful as ever. Your fur, it's so soft."

"Hmph. Nice try, Oscar. Don't even think about it. Luna is right in there. If she had any sense, she'd scratch your ears off."

"Still as feisty as ever," Oscar said, but he backed down and threw me a contemptuous glare. "You're late. I want to see my kits."

I'd never gotten used to the officious tom, and what Luna saw in him was completely beyond me. Razzy left Oscar, flipping her tail at him before joining Gus and whispering in his ear. Gus never took his green eyes off the tom, and still growled every few seconds. I hurried to unlock the cabin, revealing Rudy, standing in the doorway, his eyes full of worry.

"What's going on out here?"

"Nothing," Razzy said. "Let's get to our cabin. I'm tired."

She stalked off the short distance to the cabin next door and sat at the door, staring at Hannah. My friend laughed and shook her head.

"Well, I guess that's that. See you in the morning, Eden."

She wrapped me in a hug while Ben gave me a friendly nod before scooping up Gus. Oscar huffed out a sound that could've passed for a snort in a human and watched them go.

"If you need anything, let me know," I said. "Did you have fun, Rudy?"

His eyes still held a worried look as he nodded slowly.

"I did, but... Well... I guess we can talk about it tomorrow."

He headed off, giving Oscar an unfriendly look and leaving me wondering what he'd wanted to say. I let Oscar in and winced as the volume of meows increased as soon as the kits spotted him. My night would not be a quiet one, but I wouldn't have it any other way. Besides, with the wildflower safari kicking off in the morning, the chances of me sleeping were low, anyway. I closed the door and smiled. At least my friends were finally here.

Chapter Four

Morning came quickly, but I'd slept better than I thought I would. I got up before the sun, making sure all the kittens were settled and Jasper and Luna had everything they'd need for the long day. I wasn't sure when we'd be back, but I knew it would be later than usual. Jasper shifted as I made the bed.

"You're going to be fine, Eden," he said, nuzzling my hand as I smoothed back the comforter.

I stroked his head and hoped he was right. My nerves felt jangly as I refreshed their water and food bowls. The kits were curled against Luna while she bathed them one by one, taking extra care with the girl kit. I leaned against the counter, smiling at the domestic scene.

"That Rudy is a well-mannered cat," Jasper said, breaking the silence. "Given his early life, it's remarkable he turned out so well balanced. Hannah is an excellent human."

"She is. Did you enjoy chatting with him last night?"

"I did. He took a liking to the kits. He's patient for such a young tom."

Luna murmured as she got comfortable in her padded bed. The girl kitten squeaked before settling back down.

"All right everyone, I'll be back later. I asked Wendy to check in to make sure you've got everything you need."

Jasper shook his grizzled head.

"We'll be fine. You worry too much."

I heard Charlie's familiar knock and hustled over to let her in.

"Good morning," she sang out. "All ready for the big day?"

I grimaced, but nodded.

"I hope so. I want to look at the bus and check on the snacks I wanted to bring, just in case. The guide is providing the picnic, but you never know how hungry people will be."

"I'll check on the snacks while you check on the bus. By the time you get back to the dining hall, I'll have everything ready," Charlie said, walking over to coo over the kittens. "They're getting so big! Growing like little weeds."

A qualm worked its way through my stomach as I remembered Fig's words. It was almost time for the kits to leave and I wasn't ready for it. I pushed that thought aside. I had more than enough to worry about today without adding that to it. That would be a discussion for another day. I grabbed my bag, kissed Jasper and headed out, nearly bumping into Hannah.

She laughed and grabbed my arm to keep me from tipping over.

"Sorry! I didn't mean to sneak up on you," she said, stepping aside to reveal Rudy. "I've got a special request, if it's okay."

"Of course. What do you need?"

"Is it okay if I stay behind today, in your cabin?" Rudy asked, his tone shy. "I'll be on my best behavior."

I glanced at Hannah, who shrugged, and I nodded.

"Of course, Rudy. The more the merrier. Jasper was just saying what a fine young cat you are."

Rudy's chest puffed up with pride and he glanced up at Hannah, who beamed back at him. Charlie stepped aside as Hannah unclipped Rudy's harness and let him in the cabin. The kits started meowing as they spotted their new favorite friend. Jasper's eyes met mine as he shook his head.

"Well, it won't be dull while you're gone."

I waved and shut the door. Charlie headed off to check on the snacks as Hannah fell in next to me.

"Where are we headed?"

"I want to check on the bus before breakfast. I'm so nervous I feel like I need to keep moving."

"I'm so excited to see the wildflowers. It's been a while since Ben and I went on a hike with the cats. That's all Razzy and Gus were talking about this morning. They're so excited. It's so cool you made sure they could come along."

"Is Rudy not a fan of hiking?"

Hannah's face folded into a frown, and she looked down.

"He loves it. I'm not sure why he wanted to stay behind. It's not like him. I suppose it's the novelty of the kittens. Has Luna given them their names yet?"

"No, she's waiting for something. I'm uncertain what it is. I feel a little silly calling them boy and girl kits, but she was adamant about it."

Hannah nodded as we walked up to the giant bus parked in front of the resort. Mr. Marsburg had spared no expense. The sleek blue sides of the coach gleamed in the early morning sunlight.

"Wow, this is quite a rig. How does it open?"

I let out an embarrassed laugh as I realized I didn't know.

"Whoops. I probably should've figured that out. Well, it looks nice. I'm sure it's going to be okay. Carl must have the keys."

"It will be fine," Hannah said, looping her arm through mine as we headed back to the cabins. "You know, I remember Razzy saying something about names of kittens. I think their mothers give them something she called a 'heart name' that is very special. It's rarely shared with humans."

"Oh wow, that's so neat," I said, my steps slowing. "I didn't know. Luna said nothing like that."

"I guess it's pretty hush-hush in the cat community," Hannah said with a laugh and a rueful smile. "There's so much to them, isn't there? I feel like I could spend the rest of my life learning about them and never learn it all."

She stopped at her cabin as Ben walked out, Razzy and Gus

twining around his ankles, looping their leads all over the place. He grinned and shook his head.

"Every time."

I watched as Hannah and Ben carefully unentangled the leads while the cats waited patiently. From the mischievous looks Razzy and Gus were sharing, I gathered it wasn't entirely an accident.

"Are you ready for breakfast?"

Razzy blinked, her fur gleaming in the sunlight.

"Oh yes. I hope there's bacon. It's my favorite."

"I thought chicken was your favorite," Hannah said, taking Razzy's lead.

"For supper. Not for breakfast. Oh, I hope they have some French toast. But it won't be as good as yours, Ben. I'm certain of that."

I marveled at the love and humor that threaded through my friend's lives as we walked to the dining hall. What a gift Hannah had been given to share her abilities with Ben. Would I ever have someone like that? My thoughts flitted to Ethan before I hustled them back into place. I didn't need to daydream about him. Not today.

Breakfast was a relatively quiet affair, but I was so preoccupied with my thoughts and worries I barely tasted it. I left Hannah and Ben with promises to meet them at the bus in a few minutes while I headed back inside the resort to round up the guests and grab my backpack.

I breezed inside the lobby, trying to project a confidence I didn't quite feel, and smiled as I spotted my boss standing behind the desk with Wendy.

"Good morning," he said, his handsome face creased in a smile. "I was hoping I'd catch you before you headed out. I just wanted to say great work on getting all of this organized. I'm truly impressed."

My cheeks felt hot, and I stared at my feet for a second before mumbling a thank you. Wendy chuckled as she came around the desk.

"Where are Hannah and Ben? They're just the sweetest couple."

"They'll be meeting the rest of us at the bus. They are nice. Thank you, Mr. Marsburg, for setting everything up for them. They're super happy with the cabin."

"I owe them a lot. I hope to catch up with them before they leave."

The elevator dinged, and I turned in time to see Darlene and Milton Prescott spilling out. Her face was red, and I stiffened my spine, prepared for the worst.

"I swear, Milton. You take longer than a girl to get ready. What if we missed the bus? You know we paid good money for this trip and I don't want to be left behind."

"It's okay, Mrs. Prescott," I said, waving them over. "You're the first people here."

She smoothed the front of her shirt and looked around the lobby, finally nodding sharply.

"Good. I want to get the best seat. Did you receive our dietary restrictions? I have food allergies."

I swallowed hard and shot Wendy a look. She scurried over to the computer and pulled up the couple's room information.

"I see nothing here, Mrs. Prescott. I'm so sorry. If you can let us know what you're allergic to, I'll pass that information onto catering. I'm sure they'll be able to accommodate you."

"I swear, this place is so unorganized. You call yourself a resort? What kind of treatment is this? Milton, can you believe this?"

"No, dear."

Mr. Marsburg walked around the desk, armed with all of his considerable charm.

"Mrs. Prescott, my apologies. I'm James Marsburg, the owner. I assure you we'll do everything in our power to ensure your stay and your outing are as flawless as possible."

She blinked a few times, mollified.

"Well, that's good. I still can't believe it, though. I gave that Penny woman my list and made sure she took it down."

Wendy dug around in the drawer underneath the computer and let out a brief shout. My boss and I shared a quick look, and I suppressed heaving a sigh of relief.

"Got it! She just didn't enter it into the computer. I'll call the guide company right now, Mrs. Prescott."

"Hmph. Well, that's more like it. When can we get on the bus? I want to get going."

I checked my watch and pasted a friendly smile on my face.

"We're just waiting on everyone else. It shouldn't be long now."

"If you need anything at all, just let us know," Marsburg said. "I'll leave you in Eden's capable hands."

He made a quick escape while Darlene shot me a look filled to the brim with disbelief. The elevator dinged again, offloading a chattering group of two couples and a woman. They hurriedly joined us.

"Sorry we're late. I lost track of time. I'm Gwen and this is Gerry. It's so nice to meet you."

Gwen and Gerry had to be in their seventies, trim and bright-eyed as they looked around. Gwen's halo of white hair offset her tanned face, with a set of merry brown eyes. Gerry stuck out a hand towards Milton, who shook it with a mumble.

"And we're the Gunthers. I'm Farrah, and this is my husband, Ryan. We're so excited to be here!"

Farrah Gunther was maybe a few years older than me. Her long brown hair was tied back tightly in a ponytail. She was all smiles, but her husband looked less enthused. His neck held a few nicks from shaving, and he'd missed a tiny square of toilet paper on a cut. I thought about mentioning it, but stayed quiet.

"I'm afraid I haven't met you yet," I said, peering around the younger couple to see the woman behind them.

Her light brown hair curled softly around her round, freckled face. She was dressed simply, in a white t-shirt with jeans. I esti-mated her to be in her forties, but it was hard to tell.

"Marissa Whitmore," she said, giving everyone a friendly smile. "Is anybody else coming?"

Wendy slid my clipboard over the desk, and I took it with a grateful smile. I'd put together a list of all the attendees, the itin-erary, and the menu.

"I let the guide know about the food thing and she's going to do her best to accommodate Mrs. Prescott," she said in an undertone. I nodded and glanced at the list.

"We're just missing one more guest, Mr. Norm Fairfax."

"Present," came a shout from behind everyone. "I'm coming. I always take the stairs. Gotta stay fit."

Everyone parted to reveal a man in his sixties jogging towards us. He looked like he was dressed to play tennis instead of enjoying an afternoon hike. His white polo shirt was immaculate, and his matching white shorts revealed a set of incredibly hairy legs. A bright blue hoodie was tied around his waist.

"Can we leave now? I think we've waited long enough. We're going to be behind schedule," Darlene said, looking at her watch. "I don't want to miss anything."

I held my clipboard to my chest like a shield and nodded.

"I think we're ready. Let's head outside, everyone."

I heard Ryan Gunther mumble as he walked past.

"Oh great. Just what this weekend needed. A wild boomer. This is going to be fun."

His wife playfully swatted his arm with a giggle. Norm Fairfax fell in next to Marissa, his smile wide.

"Excited about our hike?"

Marissa mumbled something and hurried on, leaving Norm with a startled expression on his face. I couldn't help but wonder what she'd said as I ushered everyone through the doors and towards the bus. I spotted Hannah and Ben with their backpacks next to the bus and breathed a sigh of relief, grateful for their support. Carl nodded from his spot in the driver's seat while Darlene bickered with Gwen over who was going to get the front seat.

Gwen rolled her eyes and continued on, finding a seat in the middle, near where Hannah and Ben were seated. I took the other open spot at the front as the doors whooshed closed. This was it. Let the wildflower safari begin.

Chapter Five

It didn't take long for everyone to notice Hannah and Ben brought two cats on board the bus, and soon, everyone was oohing and ahhing over Razzy and Gus. I smiled as I watched Farrah stroke Razzy's head, but that quickly faded as I overheard Darlene muttering.

"I can't believe they're allowed to bring cats. Miss. Miss!"

I turned towards her, letting out a mental sigh.

"Yes?"

"Aren't there rules about bringing animals on excursions like this? I mean, who brings their cats with them on a hike? They're going to hold us back, I just know it. I will not waste my day waiting for two stupid cats."

Hannah's face flushed red as she gripped Razzy to her chest. Darlene's voice was loud, and it was obvious she'd overheard her.

"Hannah and Ben are my personal friends," I said, praying my smile wouldn't slide off my face. "Their cats are seasoned adventure cats and I'm confident they'll have no problems keeping up."

"Adventure whatsits? I've heard nothing like that. Milton? Have you ever heard of such a ridiculous thing?"

Milton mumbled something and stared out the window, his face set in its usual expression of detachment. I wondered briefly what he thought about when he answered his wife. It was obvious he wasn't listening. Marissa shifted in her seat a row back from the Prescotts, her face set.

"Well, I think it's wonderful," Gwen said, her voice carrying through the bus. "They're obviously little troopers and I think it makes it much more fun."

"You would," Darlene spat, eyeing Gwen with dislike. "I still think it's wrong."

Gerry frowned at Darlene before patting his wife's hand. I prayed we'd reach our destination as quickly as possible. I busied myself, staring at my phone, tracking our progress on my map application, and sighed. Just ten more minutes.

Finally, we turned into the trailhead and I spotted a Land Rover with a logo for Wild Peak Expeditions. We'd made it! Carl pulled the bus in and I called everyone to attention.

"Okay, folks. We're at the trailhead. We'll have a few minutes here to get acquainted with our guide, and then we'll head out on the first part of our hike. Halfway through, at Crystal Lake, we'll stop for a picnic lunch. Does everyone have their cameras ready?"

"Are there facilities here?" Marissa asked, her face pale.

"Of course. They're right over there. Let's get everyone off the bus and get organized."

I stepped out and waved at the woman waiting for us, leaning against the Land Rover. As I got closer, I realized she wasn't alone. Standing next to her was a border collie, wearing a pack vest, and a long-haired black and white cat.

"Hi, Eden, right?"

"That's me. You must be Tessa Windsor. It's great to put a face with the voice."

Tessa's long, dark blonde hair was pulled back in a ponytail, and her sunburned face was dusted with a generous helping of freckles. We'd spent ages on the phone, setting everything up, but this was the first time I'd met her. I liked her instantly.

"Same. Oh, this is Finn," she said, pointing towards the border collie, who let out a soft woof. "And this is Briar. They're my guides."

Finn came closer and sniffed my hand, giving me a gentle lick. Her brown eyes practically glowed with intelligence. Briar surprised me by leaping onto Finn's back and giving my hand a friendly bump.

"Oh wow!"

"They do that all the time. Finn doesn't mind. Whenever Briar gets tired, she hitches a ride on Finn. I got her that vest so Briar's claws won't dig in. These two girls are fast friends."

"Did you get the message about food allergies? I'm so sorry I missed that. I hope it's not a problem."

Tessa waved her hand.

"Not at all. I stopped and picked up a few things just to make sure she'd have plenty to eat. It will be fine."

I stroked Briar's silky fur before remembering I had a job to do. Darlene was standing directly behind me, arms folded across her sizable chest, glaring.

"Okay, everyone. Let's get lined up. Is Marissa back?"

I searched the small crowd for Marissa but didn't see her. Hannah and Ben hung back, and I could tell Hannah was worried. She focused on the dog and cat, and I turned to Tessa.

"Are Finn and Briar okay with other cats? I've got two in my group."

"Of course. Here, have them come over and we'll make sure everyone gets along before we leave."

"Oh, for Pete's sake, can this get any sillier?" Darlene griped, hands on hips now. "If these people would leave their dang pets at home, this wouldn't be an issue. We're wasting precious time."

I motioned for Hannah and Ben and they came over, skirting around the other hikers in the group. Razzy and Gus were in their arms, their eyes wide with curiosity as they looked at the dog and cat.

"Razzy, Gus, I'd like you to meet Finn and Briar," I said, stepping back.

Briar's eyes lit up when she saw the two felines and Finn let out another soft woof before dropping into a playful stance, unseating Briar. The cat gave Finn a glare before walking over to stand in front of Hannah and Ben.

The cats sniffed noses, and I overheard their whispered conversation as they got acquainted. I glanced at Finn, wondering if I could understand dogs, too, but either she kept quiet, or my gift didn't work on canines. I smiled though as noses were sniffed, a tail wagged, and Tessa smiled.

"There. We're all friends now. Eden, do you mind if I go through my spiel?"

"Not at all. Wait, let me make sure all of my group is here."

Marissa still hadn't shown up, so I headed towards the restrooms. She popped out right as I walked up, her face flushed.

"Sorry. I'm coming."

"No worries. Is everything okay?"

"I'm fine."

She didn't elaborate and hustled ahead of me, head down. As soon as Marissa joined the group, Tessa began speaking.

"Alright, everybody. Thanks for coming with us today. We've got a big day planned, and hopefully you're all wearing some good quality shoes. The hike won't be too treacherous, and I've got water stations up at checkpoints throughout the journey. We'll be seeing a wide variety of flowers and I'll make sure everyone has plenty of time to photograph them. Does anyone have questions?"

Surprisingly, everyone was quiet, and Tessa gave us a wide smile.

"Alright, then, let's go!"

She led the way, with Finn at her side. Briar walked with Razzy and Gus, their tails twining together. I wished I was close enough to overhear them, but from the looks on Hannah and Ben's faces, they were having a great time. I shouldered my backpack and brought up the rear after making sure everyone was accounted for. Norm lagged back, joining me.

"So, you're the one who came up with this idea, huh? First time I've ever done something like this, but it seemed like a good way to get out and meet people."

"I am," I said, nearly tripping over a rock on the trail. "Have you ever stayed at Valewood before?"

"My wife and I would come every summer, back when the kids were young. It was our getaway time. The kids are all in college now, and my wife passed away five years ago. This is the first trip I've taken without her. She always loved wildflowers. In a way, it's like she's here with me."

His face was drawn into stark lines as he looked into the distance. My heart broke a little, imagining what it must be like for him.

"Oh, I'm so sorry to hear that. I'm glad you came with us. It's a beautiful way to remember her."

"I like that," he said, a ghost of a smile flitting across his face. "I should do more of the things she loved. I never really had time for all of that. It was always work, work, work. Our little annual trips were the one time I focused on her. I wish I'd done it more. Cancer's a terrible thing, you know. That's why I work so hard to stay fit. Before Maria died, I was fifty pounds overweight, pre-diabetic, and falling apart. I got healthy so I could take care of her. I was tempted, after she died, to go back to my old ways, but the kids need me, you know? I always thought I'd be the first one to go."

I didn't know what to say, but I smiled and patted his arm. Strains of a loud voice complaining wafted back to me.

"Where is she? I need to talk to her."

Norm looked ahead before turning with an apologetic grimace on his face.

"Uh oh. I think she means you."

I hustled forward towards the front of the line where Darlene was waiting, tapping her foot.

"There you are! Where were you? Aren't you supposed to be taking care of us?"

"I was bringing up the rear, Mrs. Prescott. What did you need?"

"These bugs are terrible! I can't believe the resort would send us out completely unprotected. We were not warned that we'd be feasted upon."

I dipped a shoulder to get my pack off, glad I'd thought ahead, and packed a few things for just this sort of scenario.

"I've got some bug spray in here," I said, while I rummaged around, finally closing my hand over the bottle. "Here you go."

She took it and glared at the label before sneering at me.

"Do you really think I'm going to put poison on myself? Really? It's the twenty-first century. Haven't you heard what that chemical cocktail can do to the human body?"

"Oh, for crying out loud," Gwen said, rolling her eyes while her husband looked at the ground. "It will be fine. Use the darn spray."

Everyone else milled around while Darlene pitched her fit, and my cheeks felt hotter than the sun as I realized everyone was staring at me. Hannah shot me a sympathetic glance and cleared her throat.

"If you use it correctly, it shouldn't be too risky," she said, moving through the crowd to stand next to me. "Look, this doesn't contain DEET, if that's what you were worried about."

"And who are you? Are you a doctor? I don't think so. I've done my research. I simply cannot believe the resort would subject us to this type of treatment."

I felt fur brush my leg and looked down to see Finn leaning against me, wagging her tail gently. I put my hand on her head and felt calmer, but I still didn't know what to do. Tessa joined us and looked at the bottle I was holding.

"I've got the same stuff. I'm sorry, I didn't think to grab another kind. It should be just fine, though. You could just spray some on your clothes."

Darlene looked like she was settling in for a good rant, and I felt about two inches tall. Marissa stepped forward, holding a bottle of lotion.

"I've got some natural stuff, if that will help. I bought it at the organic store back in town."

Darlene ripped it out of her hand and scrutinized the label before huffing.

"Well, that's more like it. Thank you."

She liberally applied the lotion all over her arms and tucked the bottle into her bag, even though Marissa stood there with her hand out.

"Okay, everyone," Tessa said, pasting on a bright grin. "Let's keep going. We're about a half an hour from the first lake. We'll find a wide variety of flowers there and it's the perfect spot to get some splendid pictures."

The group followed her lead and Finn gave me a short woof before scrambling after Tessa. Somehow, her presence had helped, but I didn't know how. I watched as Razzy, Gus, and Briar followed Ben and Hannah and waited again for everyone to pass me until I was at the back. Norm had moved up next to Marissa, leaving Farrah and Ryan just ahead of me.

"She's gonna be like that the whole trip. You realize that, right?" Ryan said. "I don't know why you wanted to come on this darn thing so much."

"It will be fine," Farrah said, looking around. "Oh, look at that! Indian paintbrush. I've got to get a picture."

She dashed ahead while Ryan grumbled. He caught me listening in and gave me an unfriendly look that set my teeth on edge.

"People like Darlene should just be put out of their misery. They ruin things for everyone."

I blinked, startled by his vehemence, but I had no response. He made a rude noise and continued on, calling for his wife. I trudged ahead, full of serious doubts about this so-called great idea. I'd envisioned a happy excursion, filled with flowers and good times. So far, it seemed like everything was going wrong.

Chapter Six

As we got further into nature, my mood lifted. Even Darlene had kept the complaints to a minimum, but she kept scratching at her arms, cursing the local bug population. I steered as clear of her as I could at our frequent photo stops and hung back, admiring the way Tessa led the group. She was incredibly knowledgeable about the area. I'd already promised myself that I was going to buy a book on the local flora and fauna when I got back to the resort.

It felt good to stretch my legs, and the temperature was just perfect. Even though the sun was beating down, the cooling breeze kept me from overheating. As we rounded the bend on the trail, I felt peace return to my soul. A little chirp at my feet alerted me to Briar's presence, and I smiled at the pretty cat.

"Razzy says you and her humans talk to cats. Is that true?"

I checked to make sure I was far enough away from the stragglers that I couldn't be overheard.

"It is, Briar. You have a lovely voice."

She really did. It was not what I expected, husky and low in tone.

"Thank you. That's very nice of you," she said with a polite blink. "Tell me more about this clowder at the resort. I've always been fascinated by feral cats."

I spent the next few minutes filling her in on Fig, Willow, Ollie, and, of course, Jasper. She nodded, strolling gracefully next to me. Her energy never seemed to flag.

"Are you used to hiking?"

"Oh yes. That's our job. We're guides. Finn, of course, has more than I do, but she's a good sport."

I smiled at the notion of cats and dogs having a job, but it was clear Briar took it seriously. I'd learned so much about cats in the past few months. It no longer felt odd to think of Briar as being gainfully employed.

"Does Finn talk, too? I don't mean to be rude," I said as she turned a sardonic look in my direction. "I've never been able to talk to dogs, not like I can with cats. She helped me back there when I was feeling upset."

"Finn does that. She has a special way about her. We have our way of communicating. She's quite intelligent. For a dog."

I waited for her to elaborate, deeply curious about the inter-communication between species, but Briar remained mum. Instead, she said something that took me off guard.

"All is not right with your group. Finn senses something and she's worried. I agree. I feel something bad coming."

I stopped in the middle of the trail.

"What do you mean?"

Briar gave a kitty shrug before continuing.

"I can't put my paw on it, but be careful. Someone is not who they say they are. I need to get back to the front. It was nice talking with you, Eden."

She scampered ahead, long fur flowing out behind her as I followed at a much slower pace. What on earth had that meant? I was so lost in thought, I almost missed Tessa's shout. We were at the spot where we'd take our lunch. I looked around as we came into a clearing and the beauty of the lake took my breath away.

The alpine lake was almost the same blue as the water I'd seen in pictures of glaciers, and the meadow was dotted with so many kinds of wildflowers, it looked as though we'd stumbled into a painting. I caught up to the group and found Hannah and Ben.

"There you are. I was wondering if you'd changed your mind and went back to the bus. Not that I'd blame you. I'd have done it if I was in your shoes."

Ben chuckled before turning around to take in the view. Razzy pawed at Hannah's leg, and she bent down to scoop her up.

"What do you think, baby girl? It's beautiful, isn't it?"

"Gorgeous. What's for lunch?"

"That's my girl," Ben said, ruffling the fur on Razzy's head. "Priorities, right? It looks like everyone is getting set up over there. Let's go get our spot."

I stayed put, staring at the lake for a few more moments before I realized I should help Tessa. I jogged ahead and met her at a large stump where she'd set up an impromptu table with a cooler. I blinked in surprise.

"Did you haul all of this up here?"

"No," she said, her freckled face splitting into a grin. "I've got a few helpers that go ahead on these hikes and get everything set up. They're true gems. I made sure they grabbed the special food for Darlene."

Finn barked a sharp sound, and Tessa glanced down.

"What's wrong, girl? Are you hungry? You know I'll share my lunch with you. I always do."

Finn let out a low whine and turned in place, while Briar looked on from her spot on the stump. Briar's yellow gaze met mine, and I shivered as I remembered what she'd said earlier. I shook off the feeling and helped Tessa get everything laid out. The table practically groaned under the weight of the food. She'd brought a variety of sandwiches, cold fried chicken, potato chips, some chilled salads, and plenty of drinks for everyone. I clapped my hands and motioned for everyone to join us.

Predictably, Darlene shouldered her way into the front of the line, completely ignoring the dirty look Gwen shot her as she trod on the older woman's foot.

"Where's mine? I want nothing being cross-contaminated. I'm very delicate, you know."

It took all of my willpower not to snort. Darlene was one of the most robust humans I'd ever met, and the hike hadn't seemed to tax her in the slightest. It was as though the loud complaints she made gave her fuel. Tessa nodded and pointed out the containers at the back of the table.

"Right there, Mrs. Prescott. Please, go first."

Darlene heaped food on her plate, and I couldn't help but notice she included several things from the containers she professed to be worried about, but I held my tongue. Maybe she just needed to feel special. The rest of the group moved forward, and Milton passed Marissa a plate, giving her a shy smile.

"Here you go."

Marissa took it, her hand brushing his, and something passed between them that made me blush and look away, uncomfortable. I waited until everyone else had taken their fill before grabbing a plate and settling down next to Hannah and Ben. Gus popped his head around Ben's back, his tufted ears backlit by the sun hitting the lake.

"That smells good, lady."

Razzy sniffed the air and licked her muzzle.

"Fried chicken. I'm in heaven."

Tessa sank down next to me, folding her lanky frame into a cross-legged position while she balanced her plate on her knee.

"This is incredible," I said, sinking my teeth into a chicken leg.

"Thanks," Tessa said, while she tossed a piece of chicken to Finn, who caught it with a snap. "I get it from a little restaurant my friend owns in Collinsville. Meggie is an exceptional cook, always has been."

"How long have you been in business?" Hannah asked as she passed out little treats to Razzy and Gus. "I'm super impressed with the tour so far. You seem to know about every single flower out there."

"And my mom said going to college for botany was a waste of time," Tessa said, winking. "I started about five years ago after I lost my job at the lab. I couldn't imagine getting into the corporate world, and I love spending time outside, so this was a natural fit."

I listened while looking over at the rest of our group. Gwen and Gerry were sitting with Ryan and Farrah. Ryan looked incredibly bored and kept tossing angry glances over towards where Darlene and Milton were standing. Norm was by himself, staring wistfully at the lake, while Marissa hung between the two groups of couples, looking uncertain.

"I'd better go check on everyone," I said, putting my plate on the ground. "I'll be back."

I brushed off the seat of my shorts and walked towards Norm, my heart going out to him as I spotted the look in his eyes. I didn't know what to say to make him feel better.

"Beautiful view, isn't it?"

"It is. Maria would've loved it."

I patted him on the arm before leaving him to his solitude, not wanting to intrude on his grief. Marissa looked up and her face flushed as I approached. I gave her a friendly smile, but she looked down, not meeting my eyes.

"Are you enjoying your lunch?"

"What? Oh. Yes, it's very good. Do you know if there's going to be a dessert?"

"I think I spotted some brownies over there at the table."

"Great. I'm going to go grab one. Thanks."

She bustled off, and I stood for a second before wandering over to Gwen and Gerry's group. Ryan glanced up at me before focusing back on his food.

"Everybody doing okay?"

"Marvelous," Gwen said, giving me a sunny smile. "I'm so glad we came on this trip. Everything has been just perfect."

"We were already hoping there's going to be another one next year," Farrah said as she got to her feet. "Are you planning on doing something for leaf peeping season? I think that would be a great hike. I bet our guide would know the best spots."

Ryan snorted loudly.

"Leaf peeping? Have you ever heard of anything so silly?"

Farrah's face pulled into a frown as two angry spots of color rose on her cheeks. She sat back down and picked at the food left on her plate. Awkwardness hung heavy in the air.

"Maybe. I hadn't even thought of it. I think it's a great idea, though. This area is so pretty in the Fall."

"I think it would be lovely, don't you agree, Gerry?"

"Absolutely."

Farrah shot the older couple a grateful glance before glaring at her husband, and I dashed away, eager to complete my rounds. I'd saved Darlene and Milton for last. Marissa walked closer, holding onto a plate with a brownie, and I noticed Darlene watching her, eyes narrowing.

"Is that a brownie?" Darlene asked, approaching with the subtlety of a charging bull. "I'll take that."

She pushed past me and took the plate right out of Marissa's hand.

"I guess she loves brownies," Marissa said, shrugging as she headed back to the table to grab another dessert.

I shook my head and went back to my little group. As much fun as the actual hike had been, I was more than ready to get back to the resort and get away from the Prescotts. I sank back down and smiled at Finn as she crept closer, belly brushing the grass.

"Finn..."

Finn glanced at Tessa before focusing back on me and creeping closer. I couldn't help but giggle as the dog flopped on the ground, exposing her tummy.

"She's fine. She's too cute. Well, Tessa, it looks like your lunch was an enormous hit. I'll have to grab a brownie."

"I've found chocolate is a great fuel, especially when you're dealing with different personalities."

Her gaze was knowing as she passed me one. I sank my teeth into the chocolate-y goodness and nearly groaned at how good it tasted.

"You're sure we can't have chocolate?" Razzy asked, as Hannah shook her head. "That just doesn't seem fair. I don't know why it's got to be toxic to cats."

A screech ripped through the air, startling a flock of birds out of the nearby trees. My heart jumped into my throat as I looked around, trying to figure out who or what had made that awful sound. It plummeted back into my stomach as I spotted Darlene clawing at her throat and making horrible sounds.

"Oh my gosh!"

I tossed my plate to the side and scrambled to my feet, hurrying over to the Prescotts. Milton was standing there, frozen, a look of horror on his face as his wife sank to her knees, clutching her throat. I reached for her arm, calling her name, watching in horror as her face swelled. Ben rushed up, barking orders, Hannah right behind him.

"She's going into anaphylactic shock. Do you have her EpiPen?"

He held his hand out to Milton, who still looked on in horror, locked in place.

"Sir! Quickly! We have little time. Where is it?"

Milton stammered, wiping his face with his hand.

"I don't know."

Everything dissolved into chaos as Ben helped Darlene to lie flat on the ground and Hannah began digging through the woman's pack. Her face was pale as a sheet as she looked at Ben.

"I can't find it."

"I'm calling 9-1-1," Tessa said, pulling a strange-looking phone out of her pack.

Hannah dumped the contents of the bag onto the ground and frantically sorted through them. I knelt to help her as Darlene made horrible sounds, her face swelling out to incredible proportions. Cries of horror from the surrounding people echoed strangely through the valley. Ben reached into his pocket and pulled out a pocket knife.

"Everyone back," he said. "I need to do an emergency trach. I need something to help her get air in. A straw, a pen, anything."

I'd seen nothing like this, but I couldn't look away as Ben carefully marked a spot on Darlene's throat. Gwen gasped as he cut into the swollen flesh, and Farrah cried out, her voice strangled.

"You'll kill her!"

"Here, I found a pen."

Hannah tossed it to him and he quickly broke it down, inserting it into the hole in Darlene's neck. Finn's fur brushed my side as she leaned against my leg. I'd never felt more helpless as I watched Darlene Prescott fight for her life. Hannah continued digging through the pile of things on the grass, but there was no EpiPen. Ben held onto Darlene's hand as she rattled a breath, the sound whistling through the pen. I waited, but no more sounds came. A hush fell over the valley as Ben felt for a pulse.

Finn put her head back and let out a long howl so mournful it made the hairs on my arm stand up. I didn't need to see Ben's face to know the truth. Darlene Prescott was dead.

Chapter Seven

Once the last strain of Finn's howl ended, I stood next to Darlene's body, locked in so many emotions, I couldn't understand what I was feeling. What had just happened? Ben began doing chest compressions while Hannah counted. Tessa stood there, her face pale, gripping her phone so hard her knuckles were white.

"Stop. It's too late."

Ben kept going, ignoring Milton's whispered words. I glanced at the man, watching as he grabbed Ben by the shoulders, shaking him.

"I said stop. She's gone. There's nothing more we can do."

"There's still a chance," Ben gritted out. "I have to keep going until the ambulance gets here. Tessa, how far out are they?"

She pulled the phone away from her ear and shook her head.

"It took us two hours to get here. Even with the four wheelers they'll bring, they're still a half hour out."

"I mean it. Stop. She's dead. She wouldn't want people touching her. Let her go."

"Dude, that's your wife," Ryan said. "He's trying to save her life."

"You're right. She was my wife. And I know what she would want. It's not this. Stop touching her!"

He clawed at Ben's hands, forcing them away from Darlene's body as Gwen gasped. Finn growled low in her chest, and Tessa reached for her, groping until her hand hit the dog's harness.

"Milton," I said, struggling to find the right words. "You don't mean that. If there's a chance she can be saved, we've got to take it. Let Ben work."

"No!"

His words exploded from his chest and spittle flew. I reared back, shaken at his tone and the expression of rage on his face. Gerry and Ryan glanced at each other before approaching, their steps hesitant.

"Calm down, man," Ryan said, licking his lips. "They're just trying to help."

"It's done. She's dead. We can't do anything else for her. Just let her be at peace. I knew Darlene. None of you did. None of you! I know what she wanted, okay?"

My chest hitched and tears sprang into my eyes as I looked down at the still form of Darlene on the ground. She wasn't a pleasant woman, but she deserved a better end than dying in a random field while everyone argued over her.

Briar walked towards me, delicately picking her way through the grass, and stopped, resting her tail on my foot.

"Interesting. He seems rather adamant, doesn't he?"

Razzy's eyes blazed at Briar's words and she joined us. Gus hung back next to Ben, his green eyes never leaving Milton's face. The big Maine Coon's fur was fluffed, making him look even bigger than usual. Ben got to his feet, towering over Milton.

The smaller man flinched and moved away, his eyes darting between Ben and the other two men who were still standing close. Marissa joined him, patting his arm before leading him away.

"How did this happen?" Gwen asked, her lined face streaked with tears. "Was she allergic to bees? Was there a bee around? Was it something she ate?"

Everyone's eyes went to Tessa, and she shook her head.

"I don't know. I got the list from the resort on her food allergies and I made sure all of her food was kept separate. Nothing like this has ever happened before."

"Here," a gruff voice sounded behind me. "You can cover her with this. The, um, flies..."

I turned and saw Norm holding out the hoodie he'd tied around his waist. I took it from him and passed it to Ben, who gently laid it over Darlene's top half. Farrah began whimpering, and I felt like joining her as Darlene's death sunk in. Somehow, seeing her covered brought it all home. One of my guests was dead and there was no bringing her back. This excursion was a disaster, and I didn't know what to do. I glanced at Hannah, and she gave me a brisk nod before taking control of the situation.

"Okay, everyone, we need to stay calm. Tessa, are you still on the phone with the dispatcher?"

Tessa nodded.

"Yes, I'm on hold. I've told her what happened. They're sending out law enforcement. It should be another twenty minutes before they reach us. I sent a GPS pin to our location."

"That's good," Ben said, hands on his hips. "We need to leave everything, just as it is for the police. They're going to want to investigate."

"Investigate?" Ryan asked, folding his arms across his chest. "Why? She had an allergic reaction and died. It's not like one of us killed her or anything. And who died and made you king? Why are you ordering us around?"

Farrah made a wordless sound and put her hand on her husband's arm.

"Ryan..."

"I used to be a detective," Ben said. "I'm familiar with protocol."

"Used to be? Let me guess, you got fired for trying to impersonate an EMT."

Ryan's face was a splotchy red mess as he stared at Ben. Hannah's eyes narrowed as she sprang to Ben's defense.

"He did everything he could to save her."

Everyone started talking loudly at once and part of me wanted to cover my ears, hide, and pretend none of this had happened.

"Enough," I said, shouting to be heard. "This isn't doing anyone any good. Ben's a professional and his advice is sound. We don't know what killed Darlene. We have to keep our heads."

Hannah shot me a proud smile as the shouting subsided into mutters. Farrah led Ryan a short distance away, and they whispered, heads bent together. I drew in a shaky breath as the sound of engines filtered through the forest. Tessa spoke into the bulky phone she was holding and signed off, tucking it away into her pack. She noticed me watching and gave me a tight smile that didn't quite make it to her warm brown eyes.

"Satellite phone. I always pack one just in case we're in an area without cell service and there's an emergency. I wished I'd packed an EpiPen, too."

Finn woofed and leaned against Tessa's leg, Her hand went to the dog's back, stroking the soft fur. A four wheeler shot out of the trees and bounced along the meadow and two more followed in its wake, at a slower speed.

The engine cut off and the bulky man behind the wheel swung a leg over the machine, hitching up his duty belt as he stood. His wide shoulders blocked out the view of the trees behind him as he tilted his head to the side, staring at us.

"I'm Deputy Tucker. Where's the dead woman?"

Gwen's sharp intake of breath sounded like a gunshot in the now quiet meadow. Whoever this deputy was, he was certainly direct.

"Over here, Deputy," Ben said, striding forward, hand out. "Ben Walsh."

They stood, sizing each other up for a split second. While Ben was just as tall as the man in front of us, he was much leaner. Tucker had the frame of someone who'd played on the defensive line in college, and hadn't stopped eating like he was still competing. He didn't shake Ben's head, bumping him slightly with a shoulder as he brushed past, nodding at Tessa as he walked to Darlene's side.

"Tessa."

"Jace."

The tension between the two of them was palpable. I shared a glance with Hannah, who shrugged, but her eyes were keen as she looked at the two of them.

"Who covered her?"

"I did. The flies were congregating."

Roberts peeked under the hoodie and grimaced before putting it back in place. He turned and looked into the treeline where more four wheelers appeared.

"Alright. Suppose you want to tell me why the corpse has a hole in its neck? Which one of you stabbed her?"

"Jace, for crying out loud," Tessa ground out. "Have a little respect. I told the dispatcher what was happening, and you know dang well she wasn't stabbed. She had an allergic reaction. Ben tried to save her."

"Well, I guess it will be up to the coroner to see if that's true. I want everyone to line up over there," he said, pointing back towards the table. "Let the professionals work."

For a moment, I thought Ben was going to say something, but he frowned and turned away, leading us back to the table. Once again, I brought up the rear as the cats scampered ahead with Finn. My thoughts were nearly as heavy as my feet as I trudged through the grass. Norm slowed his steps to match mine.

"It's not your fault, you know."

I glanced at him and tried to smile, but fell short. Very short.

"I know, but I still feel responsible. She was one of our group. It was my job to keep her safe. And I failed."

Shame clogged my throat, cutting off my words, and I hung my head.

"Nonsense. You can't control everything, you know. Sometimes, bad things happen. Trust me, I know first hand. You did everything you could."

Had I? I couldn't help but replay everything that happened as I joined everyone else clustered around the remains of our lunch. I automatically began picking up the discarded plates, but Hannah came over and put her hand on my arm.

"I'd leave those, Eden. I know it's probably just an allergy, but they may need to test the food."

"What? You don't think..."

Her words made sense, but my brain didn't want to comprehend them. What was she trying to say?

Hannah shrugged and looked back towards where Darlene's body was stretched out in the grass.

"Something doesn't feel right. Razzy said something..."

She turned to see if anyone in the group was listening. I lowered my voice and leaned close.

"Briar said the same thing. She said Finn sensed something, but she didn't go into detail."

"We'll have to wait and see what the autopsy says."

I looked around for the cats and spotted them, clustered around Finn. The dog was staring, much like we all were, at the deputy and the coroner. I wished I had their superior hearing so I would know what they were talking about down there. Ben joined us, his hand going to Hannah's back. She leaned against him and looked up, her heart in her eyes.

"You did your best, hon," she said. "I still don't understand why she didn't have her EpiPen on her. As much as she talked about her allergies, I figured she'd have one."

"It's strange."

"We were just saying..."

She trailed off as Tessa joined us. The guide's face was still pale, making her freckles stand out. She looked as shaken as I felt.

"Out of all the deputies in this county, they had to send him. I'm sorry he was such a jerk to you, Ben. That's who he is, though."

"I take it you know each other," Hannah said.

"You could say that. We dated in college. He wasn't always this bad, but I was an idiot," Tessa said and looked at her feet, kicking a little grass. "I'm sorry to interrupt what you were saying. I over-heard, and I came over to say I agreed. The way her husband acted. All I can say is I hope that the man I love wants to fight to keep me alive. He was in too much of a hurry to declare her past hope."

I couldn't help but look at Milton as she spoke. Was she right?

Had Milton wanted his wife dead? In all the interactions I'd had with the couple, Darlene had been the dominant force, while Milton was passive. Why had he been so adamant about stopping CPR?

I was about to mention my suspicions when Tucker walked up. His face could have been handsome, but there was something mean about him. Cruel. I couldn't help but dislike him. How on earth had someone like Tessa dated a man like this? They seemed total opposites.

"While the coroner does his thing, I need statements from all of you. It looks cut and dried, but we're just dotting our i's and crossing our t's."

Ben frowned and I couldn't help but wish we'd been in Ethan's jurisdiction. I'd half expected him to appear out of the trees, ready to sort out this strange death. I sighed and waited my turn, hanging back to let everyone else go first. Hannah and Ben had their heads bent together, and I backed away to give them a little privacy.

Milton went first, Marissa never leaving his side. The faded man mumbled his way through his account of the incident before Marissa led him away. Roberts moved onto Norm, while everyone else waited, clustered into little knots.

"Finn says something smelled wrong about that woman."

I turned at Briar's husky voice and crouched down as Razzy and Gus crowded close. I looked around for Finn and spotted her back at Tessa's side.

"What?"

"She's right," Razzy said, nodding her head decisively. "We smelled it too. This is not a normal death. Someone killed Darlene. We're sure of it. We've been talking, and we all noticed it."

"I don't think that cop knows what he's doing," Gus said, his deep voice rumbling from his chest. "If we don't get involved, the murderer is going to get off scot-free."

My mind reeled as I turned to look at Darlene's body. Were they right? We all agreed that something didn't feel right, but murder? A shiver went down my spine as I glanced over at the group clustered near the deputy. Had someone planned to kill Darlene and set everything up?

Chapter Eight

By the time I'd answered Tucker's cursory questions, exhaustion had crept through my bones. The coroner moved Darlene's body onto a sled, attached to one of the four wheelers, and we watched, silent, as the body went past.

"All right," Tucker said, his voice loud in the valley's quiet. "You can pack everything up and head out. Mr. Prescott will ride with us to accompany his wife's body, but the rest of you will need to hike back to the bus."

"Excuse me, but shouldn't the food be saved?" Ben asked, stepping forward. "It might be necessary to determine which allergen she came into contact with."

Tucker snorted and rolled his eyes.

"Okay, Mr. Big City ex-cop. You're lucky the coroner said you did a good job with that trach, or I'd be taking you in for murdering a helpless woman. I think we know how to police our area, so why don't you just do what you're told?"

Hannah's eyes flashed as she spun on the deputy.

"Excuse me? I may be just a simple reporter, but I know you can't just discard potential evidence."

"Save me from the bleeding heart shtick, girl," Tucker said, sneering. "I know all about you. You're just like him, thinking you can boss all of us around because you're a famous reporter. We know what we're doing."

I thought Hannah was going to implode, as Ben put his hand on her arm and murmured to her. Tessa shook her head and moved closer to me.

"They're right, though. We shouldn't throw any of it away, should we?"

"No. Is there a way we can save it somehow? I can't help but feel this isn't over yet."

Her face brightened, and she nodded.

"Meggie's got a giant walk-in. We can pack everything back into these totes and I'll take it back to her to store. Great idea, Eden. We don't even need to tell anyone what we're doing. Leave no trace, and all of that."

Tucker walked over, thumbs looped through his gun belt, and gave Tessa an oily smile.

"Been awhile since I've seen you. You look good. Real good. Wanna have dinner tonight? We could catch up on old times."

"Not on your life," Tessa spat and turned away, her shoulders stiff.

"Your loss."

He strutted back to his four wheeler and drove off, spraying turf from beneath the wheels. I took a deep breath and shook my head, disturbed, disgusted and, above all, tired. We still had a two-hour hike ahead of us to get back to the bus, and we'd be carrying all the potential evidence with us. I put all of that aside and tried to put on a professional front.

"Okay, everyone. Tessa and I will get everything collected, and then we can head back to the bus. I'm so sorry about what happened."

"It's not your fault, dear," Gwen said as Gerry helped her to her feet. "We'll help clean up, too."

"I'll go get Darlene and Milton's things. I'm sure he'll want them," Marissa said, walking off towards the lake.

Hannah, Ben, and I helped Tessa get everything packed into the totes, while I told them about our plans to save the evidence. Ben nodded as he looked over the valley.

"That's a good idea. I hope we're wrong, but something tells me we'll be glad we saved everything. I can't say much for the local law enforcement, but the coroner seemed alright."

"Old Doc Hastings is a good man," Tessa said, brushing the hair out of her eyes. "You can count on him. He's been around forever. If there's something odd, he'll find it."

A thought wiggled its way through my head as I packed the last plate into the tote and put the lid on.

"But how will we know what he finds? I don't think the deputy is going to share that information with us. Can we trust him to investigate?"

"Jace is a jerk, but he's not a terrible cop," Tessa said, huffing a laugh. "As much as it pains me to say it. I'd say if something suspicious comes out, he'll investigate. I hope."

Hannah and Ben exchanged a look as Razzy let out a growl. I didn't need to be close enough to know what she was saying. I held little faith in the deputy, either.

Tessa folded up the table and stared at the pile in front of us.

"I can leave the table for my crew, but we'll need to lug these totes back to the bus. I wish Jace had left us a four wheeler."

"I'll carry the heavy one," Ben said, smiling as he hefted it. "I need the exercise."

I got everyone rounded up as Tessa grabbed the second tote and we headed back down the trail. The mood was much more somber, and the wildflowers were long forgotten as we trekked back. Halfway through, Briar hitched a ride on Finn, lightening the mood as we watched her ride the dog like a tiny cowboy. Hannah carried Razzy, and I offered to give Gus a lift when it was clear the big cat was tiring. He accepted, and snuggled close to my chest, his tufted ears tickling my chin.

"Thanks, lady," he said, his voice rumbling against my chest. "I could keep going though, if I'm too heavy."

I gave him a quick squeeze and snuck a kiss onto his forehead, comforted by his solid weight.

"Nonsense. You're helping me more than I'm helping you."

The hike seemed twice as long as it had on the way up, but finally, the parking lot came into sight. Gus hopped down and joined Razzy, their tails twining together. Ben helped Tessa load everything into her Land Rover, while the guests dragged themselves onto the bus.

"I'll get these to Meggie right away. How will I know how long to keep them?" she asked.

"We'll be in touch," Ben said. "It shouldn't take long for the autopsy report to come in. If it's what we're thinking it is, I have a feeling we'll all be hearing from the deputy before long."

I knelt down and gave Finn an impulsive hug while her feathery tail wagged. I'd never been much of a dog person, but there was something special about this border collie. She woofed softly and licked my cheek. Briar came over and sat, tilting her head to the side.

"It was nice meeting you, Eden. We hope you'll see this through."

She blinked slowly before she turned and leapt into the Land Rover. Finn was right behind her and I stood, feeling much older than I was. Tessa shifted her feet while Hannah and Ben said their goodbyes and got on the bus.

"I'm sorry all of this happened," Tessa said, as she shoved her hands into her pockets. "I feel somehow responsible."

"It wasn't your fault. Hopefully, we're wrong, and it was just a tragic case of an allergy attack that went wrong. You did everything you could, Tessa. I hope we'll see each other again."

"Me too."

She gave me a quick hug before I turned and got onto the bus, nodding at Carl. I sank into the seat right behind him as we headed out of the lot. Once we were on the road, he glanced over his shoulder.

"Sorry, Eden. I know how important this was to you. Is there anything I can do?"

Carl's kind words nearly brought tears to my eyes as I shook my head. I sniffed hard and found my voice as he focused back on the road.

"No, but I appreciate it, Carl. How did you find out? I should have called you, but I didn't even think about it. I'm sorry."

"It sounds like your hands were full enough. I was napping when I heard the sirens. I knew right away something had happened. I talked to an officer, and he filled me in. I was worried sick something happened to you, but I saw Milton was with the coroner and I knew you were okay. It was that one woman, huh? The, um..."

"Yes, Mrs. Prescott. Milton went with the cops. I didn't even think about how he's going to get back to the resort. The poor man. To lose his wife in such a terrible way. Do they have any children?"

I shook my head, realizing I knew next to nothing about most of the people on this bus. If we were right, and Darlene's allergy attack had been provoked, was one of them a murderer?

"I don't know. I didn't ask."

Carl nodded, and I glanced up at the mirror at the front, over his head. Gwen was resting her head on Gerry's shoulder, obviously exhausted from the events of the day. Marissa sat by herself, staring out the window. Ryan had his head tilted back, snoring loudly, while Farrah stared at her phone. Norm was clear in the back, head resting on his hand, very much alone. And Darlene's bag was on the seat right behind me. Marissa must have left it there after gathering their things. Hannah and Ben were a few rows back, whispering and glancing around. Razzy and Gus must have been stowed in their carriers out of sight. They were the only ones I knew I could trust.

"You don't think the husband will sue, do you?"

I looked back down at Carl and swallowed hard. I hadn't even thought about that. My great idea to bring new business to the resort had failed massively. The last thing we needed was a lawsuit.

"I don't know. I hope not."

"The guide provided the food, though, right? If anyone is going to get sued, it would be her."

"I suppose you're right. She saved all of it, though. She's going to store it at her friend's restaurant. I guess if it comes down to it, they'll be able to find out what she ate that caused the reaction. We supplied the allergy list to Tessa, but it was a little late. I suppose something might have slipped through."

"Well, I wouldn't worry about it too much," Carl said, his eyes kind as he glanced at me. "If anyone's gonna have liability, it will be the guide, not the resort. Maybe she screwed up and wasn't telling the truth about getting the right food."

That didn't ring true. But then again, how well did I know Tessa? She seemed like a great person. Someone I would want to be friends with. And her animals were great. But could I trust her? I just didn't know. I remembered what Briar had said, her warning that something wasn't right. That happened early on, before we'd even stopped to eat. Had she been trying to tell me something?

It was all just too much. I sank back in my seat and put my head back, closing my eyes. I'd experienced a lot over the past year. My murderous ex-boyfriend holding me and Hannah hostage. Three different deaths at the resort. But I'd seen nothing like what happened to Darlene Prescott. I hoped I never would again. Why hadn't she carried an EpiPen? Why had Milton refused to let Ben continue CPR?

Several questions swirled in my head as we drove through the fading light, back to the resort. Even though I loved this road, with its impressive backdrop of soaring mountains, green pines, and rugged landscape, the only thing I saw was Darlene. I owed it to her to find out what had caused her death. And if it wasn't just a tragic mistake, I would see it through, just like Briar asked. No matter where the path led.

Chapter Nine

Once we were back at the resort, I ushered everyone out of the bus and followed them into the resort, while Hannah and Ben headed for their cabin. The doors whooshed open, revealing the lobby, where Charlie and Wendy were waiting, wreathed in smiles. I made a nervous hand gesture, which went unnoticed.

"Hi everyone! Did you have a good time?" Wendy asked, bustling around the front desk. "I can't wait to see the pictures everyone took of the wildflowers."

I pushed my way around the crowd and shook my head, trying to cut her off. Charlie frowned as she looked at me and tilted her head to the side in an unspoken question. I shook my head again before turning to face the group.

"I'm sorry about what happened. The deputy said he would be in touch if he had any more questions, and asked that everyone stay for at least a few more days. If you hadn't already planned on staying on that long, we will of course be comping any extra days."

Gwen and Gerry gave me a weak smile before Gwen patted me on the arm and headed towards the elevator.

"Not your fault, dear. You've done a remarkable job. We're quite impressed."

Norm gave me a quick salute before walking towards the stairs, while the younger couple followed Gwen and Gerry.

"If she was still alive, you know dang well she'd be demanding a refund since she was inconvenienced."

"Ryan!"

Farrah's voice dripped in horror as she spun to face her husband. He gave a one-shoulder shrug and moved around her.

"If you ask me, she got what she deserved. She's probably complaining about the state of the pearly gates right now, knowing her."

The elevator doors mercifully slid shut, blocking out the rest of their conversation. Someone cleared their throat, and I spun to see Marissa standing there, holding Darlene's bag.

"Where should I put this? I wanted to make sure Milton got it, but I don't know when he'll be coming back. Have you heard anything?"

"No, I haven't. You can leave it here at the front desk and we'll make sure he gets it when he gets back."

"Okay. Well, thanks for the trip. I still enjoyed myself."

Marissa headed towards the elevators and punched a button, staring at her phone. I turned slowly and saw twin looks of horror on Charlie and Wendy's faces. My shoulders slumped as I put my head down on the front desk.

"Oh, my gosh. Did that man say someone died?"

I groaned my answer to Charlie and forced myself upright.

"Darlene Prescott died during our lunch break at the lake. It was awful, Charlie. I've seen nothing like it before."

"Did she... drown?" Wendy asked, her hand creeping up towards her mouth in horror.

"No. It looked like an allergic reaction. Ben did everything he could to save her, but it didn't help."

"Oh no, the food allergies. Did I do something wrong?" Wendy asked, her voice laced with panic. "Did I forget something on the list? Oh God, is it my fault she's dead?"

"No, Wendy. I don't think so. Wait, do you still have that list?"

She rushed behind the desk and opened the drawer under the

computer, thrusting the slip of paper towards me. Penny's writing was precise, much like the woman herself, and it was easy enough to read. I scanned through it once and then again, disbelief making my mouth fall open.

"Oh, this is weird. Look at this," I said, holding out the list towards both of them. "Shellfish, octopus, mollusks... what's a mollusk?"

"I think those are like mussels and clams," Charlie said, leaning closer. "What else is on there?"

"Pine nuts and mushrooms."

"Wow, it would be really hard to be allergic to all of those things."

I shook my head and tapped the list.

"But that's the thing. Tessa served fried chicken, potato salad, a fresh salad with tomatoes, chips, and brownies. None of the things on this list were served. How could she die of an allergic reaction?"

"Are you sure?" Wendy asked, frowning. "Maybe there was pesto in a salad. That's usually made with pine nuts. Or maybe something had mushrooms in it."

"No, I'm certain of it. I had a little of everything. The brownies had no nuts, either. I hate mushrooms and I would've noticed if there were any in the food."

"Hmmm. That's weird," Charlie said. "You should let Ethan know about this. It could be important."

A stab of sorrow lanced through me at the mention of his name. I shook my head.

"No. The hike was in the next county over, so it's not his juris-diction. The officer's name was Jace Tucker. Tessa knew him. I guess they went to school together."

"Well, maybe she had other allergies that weren't on the list," Wendy said. "Were there any bees around? Maybe she got stung. I had a classmate who was allergic to bee stings, and she always carried an EpiPen around."

"That's the other thing," I said, leaning against the desk. "If she had bad allergies, wouldn't she carry one around? Hannah checked her bag and there was nothing in there. If there had been, we could've saved her."

Charlie eyed the giant tote bag on the counter where Marissa left it and raised an eyebrow.

"This is her purse, right? It's huge. Maybe it was tucked in a pocket or something."

Curiosity warred with my abhorrence of touching a dead woman's things and quickly won. My fingers twitched before I opened the bag and peered inside.

"Hannah dumped it on the ground. It doesn't look like there are any pockets."

"Well, maybe in the heat of the moment, she missed it," Wendy said, shrugging. "They're pretty small. My classmate kept hers in a pocket."

We glanced at each other, and Charlie shrugged.

"Wouldn't hurt anything just to double check. Here, we can empty it on the table."

I glanced towards the door, feeling absurdly guilty. What if Milton walked in and found us going through his wife's things?

"I'll do it," Charlie said, snagging the purse straps. "If anyone comes in, they can yell at me and not you. You've had a rough enough day."

She took the purse over to the back table behind the desk and carefully upended it. A tube of lip balm rolled towards the edge and I grabbed it before it could fall. We carefully sorted through a pile of receipts, a nail kit, a couple prescription bottles, candies and assorted other junk before coming up empty.

"Would she have something similar in pill form?" Charlie asked, holding up a bottle to get a better look at it. "What's Losartan for?"

"High blood pressure. My dad used to take that," Wendy answered. "What else does she have?"

I pulled out the other two bottles and held them out for her.

"Let's see. We've got Amlodipine, and Motrin."

Charlie grabbed her phone and quickly typed on it.

"Another blood pressure pill and a painkiller. Nothing about allergies."

Stumped, I began putting everything back into the bag. As I rounded up the last tube of lip balm, something seemed like it was missing, but I couldn't place it. I shook off the thought and snapped the tote shut.

"It's just so strange. The other thing was her husband...."

The doors whooshed open, and I took a guilty step away from the bag as Milton walked in, head down. He was alone and didn't look at us as he walked by. My face flushed as I realized how close I'd come to him walking in on me, accusing him of not loving his wife. Shame rippled through my chest and I stepped closer.

"Mr, Prescott?"

He stopped, eyes unfocused, before realizing who I was.

"Yes?"

"I just wanted to tell you how sorry I am about your wife. We collected her things for you. Here's her bag if you want it."

A look of loathing stole over his face, punching the breath out of my chest as he stared at the bag. Slowly, ever so slowly, he shook his head. When he spoke, his voice was hoarse.

"No. I don't want it. Throw it away."

He kept moving until he got to the elevator and punched the button with enough force I was sure it would break. Charlie and Wendy exchanged looks as an uncomfortable silence filled the lobby. The elevator ding and he stepped inside, hitting the button to close the doors immediately.

"Wow," Charlie said, popping her gum. "I guess everyone handles grief differently. Do you think we should do what he asked?"

"No," I said, shaking my head. "We need to put that in a secure spot. Wendy, can you put it in the safe?"

"Uh, sure, but why?"

"Just a feeling. There may be something in there we might need."

Charlie narrowed her eyes as Wendy took the bag from me and headed towards the back.

"You think it's murder, don't you? I can tell. You've got that look in your eye."

I stared at the elevators and shrugged.

"I don't know. But something just isn't right about all of this. I should probably tell Mr. Marsburg what happened. Carl was worried Mr. Prescott might file a wrongful death lawsuit or something."

"Hmph. Something tells me that's the farthest thing from that man's mind," Charlie said, shaking her head. "He left for the day. You could try his cellphone."

I nodded as exhaustion reared its head again.

"I'll do that. I need to get cleaned up, and then I'll call him."

Charlie's face was full of sympathy as she patted my back.

"A shower and a nap are just what you need. I'm sorry, Eden. You put so much effort into this trip."

"Thanks, Char."

I tried to smile, but it didn't feel right on my face. I gave her a quick one-armed hug before heading back outside. My steps were heavy as I walked the short distance to my cabin, craving just what she'd recommended. I wanted nothing more than to wash this entire day away and pretend it hadn't happened. I knew things didn't work that way, but for a moment, I indulged in the fantasy.

Hannah popped through her door as I passed.

"Hey, Eden. Mind if I grab Rudy? I'm sure he's going to want to hear all about what happened."

I slapped my hand to my forehead as I remembered he'd stayed behind, keeping Jasper, Luna, and the kits company.

"I totally forgot! Of course, come on in. In fact, why don't you guys all come into my cabin and we can tell everyone together? Jasper's going to want to know all about it, too."

The last thing I wanted to do was relive the afternoon, but I knew our cats would want to talk about it. They thrived for intrigue and had an uncanny ability to see things humans missed. Maybe, just maybe, they'd be able to prove our suspicions right.

"Great idea," Hannah said, her face breaking into a sunny smile. "I'll go grab Razz and Gus. Oh, and of course, Ben, too. You've got room for all of us?"

"Of course."

I opened the door and was greeted by a chorus of meows, purrs, and the general cacophony that meant I was loved and missed. It soothed me in a way that human companionship never could. I spotted Rudy, curled up with the girl kitten on the bed next to Jasper, his blue eyes bright.

"Hiya, Eden. Did you have a good day? Where's Ma?"

"She's right behind me, bringing your friends. Did everyone have a good day here?"

Luna blinked from her spot on my chair, where she'd obviously taken a break from her kittens.

"It was… long," she said, stretching in place, her ears swiveling forward.

Something passed between Rudy and Luna, and I didn't understand it. He curled his tail protectively around the kit next to him and Jasper gave me a solemn look. There was a strange undercurrent in my cabin and I didn't understand one bit of it. Hannah sang out as she walked in behind me, carrying Razzy.

"Here we are. Rudy-bug! We missed you. You won't believe what happened today."

"We witnessed a murder," Razzy said, her tone breathless as she vaulted out of Hannah's arms. "We can't prove it… yet… but I know that's what we saw."

Rudy's eyes goggled as he half-stood, bumping the kitten next to him. He gave her a quick lick of apology before hopping down to stand in front of Razzy.

"What?"

Ben crowded in, carrying Gus, and shut the door behind him.

"Keep it down guys, or they're gonna think Eden's got a zoo in here."

Everyone began talking at once as I crossed over to the bed to sit next to Jasper. He put a paw on my hand, his golden eyes full of sorrow. A rusty purr started deep in his chest as I picked him up and cuddled him close. In a moment, we'd begin airing our suspicions, but for now, I just wanted to hold my cat close.

Chapter Ten

I listened with half an ear as Hannah laid out everything that happened on our doomed hike, with frequent interruptions from Razzy. Rudy listened, his face frozen in a rapt expression, as Razzy finished the tale after huffing at Hannah for focusing on the wrong elements. I couldn't help but chuckle at the expression on Hannah's face as Razzy corrected her. I had a feeling that it was a pretty frequent occurrence.

"Ben, do you think she would've been saved if you'd kept doing CPR?" Rudy asked.

Ben was sitting cross-legged on the floor, allowing the two boy kittens to climb all over him. One was investigating the short cropped hair on Ben's head, and from the looks of it, it tickled. He plucked the kit from behind his head and held him to his chest.

"Honestly? No, I don't. But I felt like I needed to do something. It didn't feel right to give up. But she was gone. I'm certain of it."

Silence settled over the cabin like a heavy blanket, wrapping us in its uncomfortable weight. I shifted on the bed, wishing I knew what to say. I was socially awkward at best, and this situation was heavier than anything I'd experienced.

"You did everything you could," Razzy said, nodding thoughtfully. "Her soul was gone. I could feel it leave."

I shuddered as I looked at the serious cat.

"You can tell things like that?"

"Oh, yes. I've seen a few bodies in my time. None that died right in front of me, but I can sense when a soul leaves. Gus? How about you?"

"Yeah. I felt it too. Right when Finn howled. I've always heard dogs can sense things like that, too, and Finn seems to be a very sensitive dog."

"This woman, she was unlikeable?" Luna asked.

I looked over at the chair, surprised. She rarely involved herself in human complaints, preferring to focus on her kits and her daily routine. I nodded slowly before shrugging.

"I'd just met her, but from our brief interaction, she seemed like she was difficult. I don't know if unlikeable is the right word."

Razzy huffed something under her breath and I gave her a half smile.

"Okay, I'm being nice. She didn't strike me as a person who would be easy to get along with. By the time we were hiking towards the lake, the other guests were already muttering about her. The only person who was nice to her was Marissa."

"Did one of them kill her? Did they get fed up and decide they didn't want her around anymore?"

Luna's little face was serious, and I drew a sharp breath, remembering what I'd overheard from Ryan on his way to the elevator. Was it possible? Had someone snapped? Hannah cleared her throat and shook her head.

"No, I don't think so. I mean, if she'd been bludgeoned or strangled, maybe yes. But an allergic reaction? That would have to be premeditated. You'd need to know her allergies and select just the right substance. You'd have to make certain she didn't have the one thing that would save her life."

"The EpiPen," I said, almost whispering the word. "We searched her bag again, just to make sure. I went over the list of her allergies again with Wendy and Charlie, and I don't think we ate anything that was on the list."

"Wait, what?" Ben asked, his jade green eyes lighting up. "She had a list?"

"That's right. You weren't in the lobby when I was getting everyone rounded up. She made a big deal about it, and we were surprised. Penny is the one who took the booking. She did it wrong in our system and then forgot to enter the allergens in as well. Wendy found the list and called Tessa to pass along the information. Tessa went and picked up a few special things to make sure Darlene would have plenty to eat."

"What was on the list?" Jasper asked, stirring from his spot next to me.

"Shellfish, mollusks, pine nuts, mushrooms and I think octopus."

"Eww," Rudy said, wrinkling his tiny nose. "Who eats octopus?"

"I think it's a delicacy in some cuisines," Hannah said. "But I know how smart they are. I don't think I could ever eat one."

Ben crossed his arms around his knees and nodded.

"Well, we definitely didn't have any of that in our food. I guess there could've been mushrooms, but I don't remember seeing any."

"Is it possible Tessa made a mistake?" Hannah asked, putting a voice to my fears. "Maybe a dish had traces of an allergen. A seasoning or something. The chicken was amazing. I think she said her friend Meggie made it, right?"

"Yeah, she's the one with the restaurant where Tessa is going to store the rest of the food until we know exactly what killed Darlene."

Hannah and Ben exchanged a look.

"So, let's say it was an accident. If Meggie or Tessa are responsible, either could hide the evidence."

"But wouldn't the contents of Darlene's stomach prove it, anyway? That would be risky and not very smart. Tessa seemed very intelligent. I liked her," I said, shaking my head. "She seemed honest. I think if she made a mistake, she would own it."

"And she likely has insurance to protect her. Didn't we have to sign a waiver when we signed up for the hike?"

"Yep," Hannah said, digging in her pocket for her phone, unseating Razzy from her lap. "It was electronic. I've got the link in my email."

We waited while she searched through her email. I'd signed the same one, but I hadn't paid attention to any of the wording, figuring it was just standard.

"Here it is. It says that we agree we have been informed of the hazards, blah blah blah, yeah, basically it absolves Tessa and her crew from any liability."

"I still don't think she was at fault. Or if she was, it was a complete accident," I said.

"I agree. It's too risky, even with the liability. That's Tessa's entire business, keeping people safe. She has a vested interest in making sure her hikers are protected. I don't think she's guilty either."

"So, who did it? If it is murder, I mean."

"The first place we look is the spouse, in cases like this," Ben said.

Razzy stretched and let out a little chirp.

"That makes the most sense. Who else would know her allergens? Who else could dispose of the EpiPen and make sure she didn't have it? It's got to be him."

I thought about Milton Prescott. He didn't strike me as a murderer. He was much too passive, almost invisible. Had he done it? Had he finally gotten sick of his wife's demanding ways and picked a hike in the wilderness to slip her something deadly?

"So, how do we prove it?" Rudy asked, bouncing in place. "Can we get a lab to analyze the food?"

"It's not that easy," Ben said, shaking his head. "But it may come to that. We'll just have to wait to get the autopsy report."

I let out a sigh and shook my head.

"I don't think it's going to be that easy. You saw how Deputy Tucker was. I don't think he's the type to share much."

Ben smiled and got to his feet, holding out his hand for Hannah and hauling her slight frame up off the floor.

"I'll give Ethan a call. I'm sure he knows some people and can help us out. I'd like to catch up with him, anyway. It's been awhile."

There was Ethan's name again. I wanted to see him. Wanted that very much. But I wanted it to be natural, not something involved with a potential murder. Again. It seemed like the only time I ever saw him was when something bad happened. I could feel Hannah looking at me, so I focused my attention on Jasper, stroking his head. From the look in his golden eyes, he knew exactly what I was doing.

"That would be a good idea. He can probably help us," I said, tickling Jasper under the chin. "I guess until we find out what killed her, there's not much we can do."

"We shouldn't rule out the other guests, though," Hannah said, leaning back against the counter. "I think we need to keep our ears to the ground and see what we can find out."

"Won't that be awkward?" Razzy asked, her blue eyes gleaming.

"Ha, ha. You know what I mean, little girl."

"Sorry, couldn't resist. What's for supper?"

Everyone looked at me and I shrugged. Food was very far from my mind, even after the long hike and everything that happened.

"I'm sure the kitchen staff has whipped up something delicious. You guys go ahead. I think I'm going to hang out here for a little while."

Hannah frowned a little as she looked at me.

"Are you sure?"

"Yeah, I need to get these guys fed. I'll be over soon. I'm not hungry."

Hannah crossed the room and gave me an impulsive hug that nearly brought tears to my eyes. I'd grown up so isolated, with only my sister for companionship, but in the past year, I'd made friends. Real friends. People like Hannah, Ben, Charlie, and everyone else who worked at the resort. They were quickly becoming the family I wished I'd had growing up.

"Thanks, Hannah. I'll see you in a few minutes."

"We'll be there. Alright guys, let's give Eden some space and get ready to go eat."

Razzy led the way to the door, but Rudy hung back, shuffling a paw over the rug, idly picking at it with his claws. Hannah paused and looked over her shoulder, waiting for him.

"Rudy? Are you coming?"

"Yeah, there's just... Well, I don't know if it's my place, and I don't know if anyone else has noticed it, and it seems like it's super important, but I don't know if I should say anything."

Hannah swung the door closed as Rudy's words rushed out, tripping over each other on their way out. He heaved a little sigh and looked at the girl kitten. Everyone followed his gaze to where she was lying on her side, playing with Jasper's tail. Luna straightened in her chair and hopped down, her limbs stiff.

"What?"

If it was possible for a cat to blush, Rudy's cheeks would've been stained pink. He blinked at the white cat before hanging his head. I exchanged a glance with Hannah, but she shrugged.

"Go ahead, bud," Ben said, kneeling next to the Ragdoll cat, his knees popping. "Don't be shy. You're among friends."

The look Rudy shot Luna said he questioned that, but he puffed up his chest a little and looked at Ben.

"The girl kitten... Does anyone realize she's deaf?"

I blinked several times as I looked at the little kitten on the bed. It was true. Her voice was much louder than the other kittens, but I didn't know if that mattered. She didn't interact with me as much as they did, but I'd put it down to her being shy, or not as boisterous as her brothers. Was Rudy right? Luna hissed, her ears drawing back so far they looked plastered to her head as she hopped on the bed and circled herself around the kitten.

"You shouldn't say things like that. She's fine," Luna said, hissing again as she looked defiantly at Rudy. "There's nothing wrong with her."

His face pulled into a miserable expression, and he scuffed his paw again.

"I'm sorry. I'm not saying anything like that. But she can't hear. I tried several times. Look, the boy kittens, they're watching our every move, aware of what we're saying. But that's not all..."

I glanced at the kits as he trailed off. Their little eyes looked worried as they stared up at the much taller people surrounding them. Meanwhile, the little girl was still playing with Jasper's tail. I looked to Jasper for support, and he blinked slowly.

"I know. I was waiting to see if it was temporary, but I'm afraid it's not. Luna, you know. You must know."

Luna nuzzled the kitten closer to her and wrapping her in a protective paw. "She's perfect."

"Of course she is," I said, smiling. "If she can't hear, that doesn't make her broken. It just makes her special."

Fur brushed my ankle, and I looked down, surprised to see Razzy approaching. She hopped onto the bed and ignored the other queen, hissing as she sat down, giving them their space.

"She's beautiful," Razzy said, her voice quiet. "She looks like you, Luna. And she has her father's eyes. Of course she's perfect. But can she hear?"

I only knew a fraction of the reason these two queens didn't get along, and this show of solidarity from Razzy was surprising. Luna seemed taken aback, and it took her a minute to respond. When she did, I had to lean closer to hear her.

"She is. I already told Eden I wanted the girl kitten to stay with the humans. Now it's even more important. How can she live in the wild? She can't hear anything coming. She'd be defenseless. If Fig and Oscar don't agree, what am I going to do? I'd stay with her as much as I could, and I know her brothers would too, but what if... what if something happens to her?"

Luna's thin tail wrapped around her body tightly and my heart broke just a little for this brave mama cat.

"Fig will agree," Jasper said, his voice throatier than usual. "I'll recommend it myself. I've been thinking about it for weeks now."

"If I have to leave the clowder, I will," Luna said, eyes blazing. "I won't let anything happen to this precious kit. I don't care what Oscar thinks. I tried to tell him, but he won't listen. He has his own ideas."

Razzy let out a growl and shook her head.

"Toms. We'll help you, Luna. Don't worry. You're not alone."

Something passed between the two queens, words unspoken but shared. Finally, Luna relaxed and breathed out a long sigh.

"Thank you."

Rudy approached, his paws silent on the floor.

"Eden's right. She is special. And not just because she can't hear. This kit has a gift. She's not ready to share it with everyone just yet. But when she does, it will be very important."

Everyone looked at the young cat in surprise as Luna tilted her head to the side.

"I think you're right, Rudy. I've felt something, too. When I named her, with her heart name, I was certain. We'll have to see what she decides."

I was out of my depth and mouthed the phrase 'heart name' as Hannah smiled, a knowing expression on her face.

"That's a special name mama cats give their kittens," she said, seeing my confusion. "Razzy told me about it. They don't share those names with humans, so don't ask. When the time is right, she'll get a new name, one that is for everyone. But the heart's name, that's just for her."

I smiled as that little nugget of knowledge from the hidden worlds of cats nestled into my heart.

"What a beautiful thing."

Razzy gave Luna a solemn nod before hopping off the bed. The white cat looked faintly surprised but shifted her attention back to her kitten, cleaning her little ears.

"I'm starved," Razzy announced, marching to the door. "Let's eat."

The tension that had gathered in my little cabin dissipated as though by magic as everyone chuckled. Ben nodded and snapped the lead on her harness.

"Alright my queen, let's go."

Rudy hung back again, his blue eyes soft as he looked at the kits.

"They're marvelous, Luna. Truly."

She didn't look at the cat as he turned to follow Hannah, Ben, Razzy, and Gus outside. But I could tell his words meant something to the feral cat on my bed. Jasper stood and stretched.

"I find deep revelations make one hungry. Do we have any more of that leftover prime rib?"

He hopped down, moving a trifle stiffly, but given his age, still nimble. I smiled as I followed him. He'd come a long way from the failing cat I'd discovered under a bush, who wasn't sure he wanted to stay with me. I got up and prepared everyone's meals. Thoughts of Darlene Prescott and her strange death banished from my mind, at least temporarily.

Once everyone was done, I tossed on a hoodie against the chill and stepped outside, breathing the fresh air. A slight glow was all that was left of the sun behind the mountains to the west. I turned and noticed two people walking through the parking lot, their heads bent together. One of them was Milton Prescott, but who was with him? I squinted through the low light of dusk, but I couldn't make out their features. It was a woman, that much was clear. But who?

Chapter Eleven

I stared at my ceiling, trapped by the sheets I'd twisted around my body as I thrashed around in bed. What little sleep I'd gotten had been filled with nightmares involving Darlene Prescott, beasts in the woods, lurking just out of sight, and tiny kittens meowing. A quick glance outside, towards the drapes I'd forgotten to close, confirmed that the sun was coming up, but all I wanted to do was get a few more hours of sleep.

The rustling noises and tiny meows coming from the playpen told me that wouldn't happen. Jasper grumbled from his spot on the pillow next to me.

"You wiggle more than a fish."

"Sorry, Jasper. I probably kept you up all night."

He slid his head back onto the pillow, eyes firmly shut, and sighed. I tugged my legs free from the covers and sat on my bed, head in my hands. My hair was snarled into one big tangle. I'd forgotten to braid it before falling into bed. I thought back to the quiet dinner I'd shared with my friends. I'd picked at my food, ignoring Charlie and Danny's usual antics, barely even hearing them.

My cellphone trilled from its spot on the nightstand and I

grabbed for it, noticing the name on the screen. I swallowed hard and accepted the call.

"Good morning, Mr. Marsburg. You got my message?"

"Morning, Eden. I'm so sorry you had to go through all of that yesterday. From what I've heard, you did an admirable job of keeping everyone calm and getting everyone back to the resort safely."

I hadn't expected praise, but my boss was a nice man. It still felt wrong to get accolades when everything had gone so wrong.

"I'm so sorry. I had such high hopes for this event."

"It's not your fault someone had an allergic reaction and died, Eden. These things happen. I've heard from the county sheriff's office. Apparently, something interesting came up and they want to interview everyone again."

I sat up straight, heart thudding.

"Really?"

"Deputy Tucker will be at the resort by eight. I'll be coming in as well to assist with the guests and any issues that might crop up. I think it would be best to set aside the conference room, stock it with some breakfast items, and get the guests from the trip to congregate there."

I glanced at my watch. We had an hour before the deputy arrived. I'd have to wake the guests and explain what was going on.

"I'll take care of it, sir."

"Thanks, Eden. I knew I could count on you. I'll be in a little after eight."

I signed off and quickly made the bed around Jasper. He didn't move as I placed the comforter over his thin shoulders. Luna blinked at me as I went racing by, grabbing some clothes on my way to the bathroom. My thoughts jumbled around in my head as I showered, grateful once again that I'd cut my hair, reducing the time I had to spend getting ready.

I fed the cats and was out the door with forty-five minutes to spare. I paused at the cabin next door and knocked softly on the door. It took a few moments, but Hannah poked her head through, her curly blonde hair going in at least ten different directions.

"Morning, Hannah. Deputy Tucker wants to interview everyone again. We'll be meeting in the conference room at eight."

Her blue eyes brightened as she tried to get her hair in order.

"Can I help?"

I smiled and shook my head.

"No, I've got it under control. See you in a few."

As I walked into the resort's lobby, I was surprised by how confident I felt. I'd told Hannah the truth. I had it under control. I could do this. Charlie waved from the front desk, blowing an enormous bubble with her gum and popping it loudly.

"What are you doing here so early? Aren't Sundays your day off?"

I took her aside and explained what was going on. She sobered and nodded, pulling up the list of room numbers from all the guests.

"I'll call them and get them up if you want to get the conference room ready."

"Great, and then I'll get the food all set up. Are the coffee machines already going?"

"Yep, I refreshed them a half hour ago. Danny can take care of the food. I'll text him now."

I shot her a grateful glance before heading down the hallway towards the conference room. It sat just off of the main lodge sitting area where we kept the coffee pots. I used my key card to open the door and started getting everything set up. By the time I was done, I turned around to see Danny, laden with bags and boxes from the kitchen. I rushed forward to help as the wonderful smell of freshly baked cinnamon rolls wafted towards me.

"Thanks, Danny. I really appreciate this."

"Hey, any time. I still can't believe what happened yesterday. Charlie told me about it. If there's anything I can do, just name it."

I knew he meant it. Danny might be a little goofy and weirdly obsessed with potatoes, but he was a solid friend. He was helping me get all the refreshments situated when Gwen and Gerry walked in. Even though it was early, they were both bright and chipper as they took their seats.

"Good morning," I said, smiling as I stacked the cups on the table. "I'm sorry to disturb you so early."

"It's fine," Gerry said, snagging two cups and filling them from the carafe. "We're hoping the deputy will have an update on poor Darlene. What a terrible way to go. Hopefully, Milton can get some closure. Here you go, sweetheart."

He delivered Gwen her cup of coffee and she buried her nose in it, inhaling the wonderful fumes. I smiled as I watched them interact. They were the sweetest couple. The door opened again, revealing Hannah and Ben. They said their good mornings to everyone as I finished putting out the napkins and plates.

"Those look delicious," Hannah said, eyeing one of the cinnamon rolls. "I'd better save some for the cats. They were not pleased about being left behind. Especially Rudy, since he missed everything yesterday, too."

She grabbed two cups of coffee and two rolls, sliding them towards Ben. He took them with a smile and raised the cup to her before taking a sip. Gwen tilted her head and sighed a little as she watched them interact. I felt like doing the same.

Loud voices sounded from the other side of the door and it slammed open, shoved by Ryan. His short hair looked messy, and his unshaven face was tight with anger as he walked into the room.

"This is ridiculous," he said, grabbing a cup of coffee and slurping it loudly before plopping down into a chair.

Farrah tried to smile before getting her own cup and sitting next to him. She wrapped her hands around the cup and stared at the table.

"It's got to be done, son," Gerry said, his voice hearty. "Nothing to it, but to do it."

"Spare me your platitudes. And I'm not your son."

Awkward silence crowded in between everyone and I searched for something to say to dissipate it, but came up empty as the door opened again. This time it was Norm, and much like Gerry, he seemed like more of a morning person as he cheerfully greeted everyone. His eyes were bright when they met mine, and he gave me a friendly nod.

"I'm glad the front desk had my cell phone. I was out taking my morning walk when they called. So, we've got to meet with the deputy, huh? Do you know what this is about?"

"I haven't been told, but I assume it's a continuation of their investigation," I said as Marissa slipped into the room.

Her round face was pink as she scuttled to the other side of the conference table and took a seat. I gave her a friendly smile and pointed out the coffee and rolls, but she shook her head, looking down at her hands. That left just one more person before Deputy Tucker joined us.

Danny tapped my arm and drew me back into the corner of the room.

"Is it just me, or does this feel really awkward?"

"It's not just you. Thanks again for helping. You can go."

He made a face and nodded.

"I've got other stuff I can do. If you need anything or if anyone gets out of line, just call me or Trevor. We'll help."

I noticed he was staring at Ryan while he said that. While the man was definitely abrasive, rude, and thoroughly unlikeable, I didn't think he'd become violent, especially with a deputy in the room.

"We'll be fine. See you later."

Danny left and held the door open for Milton. I wasn't sure what I expected a grieving husband to look like, but Milton was all smiles as he walked in. He zeroed in on the coffee.

"Good morning, everyone. Beautiful day out there, isn't it?"

Gwen blinked and frowned slightly, but stayed silent as Milton held a running stream of commentary on the wonders of waking up in the countryside. He sat on the same side of the table as Marissa, leaving a seat in between. As he munched on a cinnamon roll, I couldn't help but wonder who he'd been walking with the night before. A loud voice in the hall heralded Deputy Tucker, and I sank into the seat next to Hannah as he entered.

"Everyone here? Good, good. I'm sorry to get you all out of bed on a Sunday morning, but there are a few things we need to wrap up. Mr. Prescott, your wife's body will be released tomorrow. You can make your arrangements for her burial."

Milton looked a little stunned.

"Oh. I didn't realize. I don't... I don't know what to do. I never thought about her dying. I always figured I'd go first. We never talked about things like that."

"Do you have any children?" Gwen asked, her face full of sympathy.

"What? Oh, no. We never had kids. Darlene had no use for them, and I guess it really didn't matter."

"Did she have any favorite music?" Farrah asked. Her husband snorted, and she shot him a glare before continuing. "When my mom arranged my grandma's funeral, she included some of her favorite songs. I know it can be overwhelming."

Marissa held up a hand.

"I can help. I had to do it for my mother. I know how hard it can be."

Milton smiled and nodded.

"Thank you. I appreciate it."

"To get back on track, I'd like to take everyone back through the events that happened yesterday, from the time you left the resort to the time Mrs. Prescott died," Tucker said, his blocky face impassive. "Mr. Walsh, why don't you start?"

Ben nodded before launching into his account. Even though I'd been practically next to them for most of the hike, the amount of detail he went into was startling. It appeared Ben noticed everything. He even remembered waiting on Marissa to use the restroom before we left the trailhead. I'd forgotten that.

One by one, we related what we'd seen and heard the day before. I went last, but I couldn't think of anything different to add. Tucker listened, but I noticed he wasn't taking notes. I finished my account, including mentioning we'd saved the food, just in case it was needed. I looked at Tucker, interested in his reaction. He frowned and nodded.

"Yes, I've already talked with Ms. Windsor. That was unnecessary. I told her to dispose of the food."

My heart sank, but I held onto a shred of hope that Tessa had ignored his instructions. It might be the only way we could prove our suspicions about Darlene's death. Tucker fell silent, looking around the room at each of us. The silence stretched to where it felt like it could snap. I breathed a sigh of relief as Tucker spoke again.

"Mr. Prescott, your wife, had a current prescription for an EpiPen. Do you know why she didn't have it with her yesterday?"

"She did? Oh, I don't know. I never paid attention to things like that. She must have forgotten it or something."

"According to her physician, she always carried it with her. After an incident when she came across an allergen at lunch with her friends, she was instructed by her doctor to have one on hand. I confirmed with her pharmacy that she renewed her prescription three months ago when her old pens expired."

I sat up straighter, convinced we were onto something. It sounded like Darlene was fully aware of the risks she faced, so why wasn't the pen in her bag?

"I see. Well, she always handled all the packing and everything for our trips. I never bothered with things like that."

"Do I have your permission to search your room, Mr. Prescott? I can get a warrant if you prefer."

Milton sat up, his fleshy body slightly quivering, and nodded furiously.

"Of course. I have nothing to hide. Please do. How terrible! If she'd only had it with her, we could've saved her."

Somehow, his response felt flat, but I hesitated to judge. Obviously, Milton and Darlene hadn't been close. I looked around the room at the various couples and frowned. Hannah and Ben were obviously devoted to each other, as were Gwen and Gerry. Farrah and Ryan seemed to have an entirely different dynamic. It was obvious Norm still mourned his dead wife, even though she'd passed years ago. Was Milton Prescott still in shock, or was he just that out of touch with his wife? I glanced at Marissa and saw she was comforting Milton, her hand on his arm.

"Great. Well, I think that's everything. We're still waiting on the autopsy report, but it looks as though this is a tragic case of an accidental death. All of you should be cleared to leave as soon as that's in tomorrow. You have my sympathy, Mr. Prescott. Miss Brooks, can you accompany me to Mr. Prescott's room?"

I started and stood, almost tipping over my coffee cup. I reached for it just in time as I nodded.

"Of course. I'll go get the manager's key from the front desk. We can meet at the elevator."

He gave me a copy of the oily smile he'd given Tessa the day before, and I cringed internally before hustling out of the room. I ran into Danny and Charlie, who stepped back quickly. Their faces were arranged in twin expressions of surprise. I couldn't resist a brief chuckle.

"Eavesdropping?"

They fell in next to me as we walked back to the front desk. Charlie shrugged and tossed her ponytail over her shoulder.

"Can you blame us? It's too bad those doors are so dang thick. I couldn't hear anything. Danny?"

"Barely a word. So, what happened? Who's guilty?"

"Charlie, I need a manager's key," I said, glancing over my shoulder. "I need to take Deputy Tucker up to Mr. Prescott's room."

"Uh oh," Danny said, his eyes bright. "You'll tell us all about it when you get back, right? The suspense is killing me."

I frowned at his choice of words, and Danny's cheeks went pink as Charlie handed me the key card.

"Geez, Danny. You can't say things like that. But, definitely, Eden. You gotta tell us what went on in there."

"I will. I'll be back in a few minutes."

I almost asked Charlie to go with me up to Prescott's room, but Deputy Tucker was already standing there, giving me a look dripping with impatience. I hustled towards the elevator and hit the button.

"They're on the top floor," I said as we waited for the elevator car.

"Have you worked here long?"

The doors opened, and I stepped inside. I noticed everyone else was hanging back, and as the doors slid shut, I noticed Marissa and

Milton standing together. Was she the one I'd seen walking with him last night?

"A few months," I said as the elevator lurched upward.

"Where'd you work before?"

"I was a staff member at Ken Brockman's estate."

He let out a low whistle as the doors opened. I led the way to Prescott's room and used the card to open the door.

"The actor? Wow! Why'd you leave? He's a pretty big Hollywood star. That might have been good for your upward momentum, if you know what I mean."

I knew what he meant, and it made my stomach roll uncomfortably as I pushed open the door and held it for him.

"I can wait out here."

"I don't mind if you watch," he said, dropping a wink that made me feel gross.

I stayed in the doorway as he walked through the Prescott's room. It looked as though a bomb had gone off inside. Women's clothes were strewn everywhere, hanging on every surface. My heart clenched as I imagined going back to a room I'd shared with someone, knowing they'd never be back to sort through their things.

Tucker stayed mercifully silent as he searched the room. I noticed he didn't find the EpiPen and my suspicions ratcheted up.

"Are you going to search their home?" I asked, unable to contain my curiosity as he joined me in the hall.

"I don't see the need to do that. She must have changed bags like you women like to do and forgot to put it in."

I let the heavy door close behind me and walked towards the elevator, questions swirling in my mind. I just couldn't believe someone like Darlene had just forgotten the one thing that would've saved her life.

Chapter Twelve

Hannah and Ben were leaning against the front desk, talking with Charlie, Danny, and Wendy as I came out of the elevator with Deputy Tucker. I rushed ahead, happy to see Hannah's face light up as soon as she saw me. She opened her mouth to say something, but Tucker spoke over her.

"Thanks for showing me everything," he said, nodding in my direction before focusing on Ben. "I pulled your background. It's a shame you left the force. You were highly respected, and on the track to success. Why'd you leave?"

Ben's chin came up as he looked at the deputy.

"It was the right thing to do. When politics and the friends of the chief matter more than the truth, it's time to move on."

"Huh. Can't say I'd make the same decision. It's your life, though. See you around."

He swaggered back through the sliding doors, and I watched him go, glad to see the back of him.

"Ugh. Just listening to him makes me want to take a shower," Charlie said, cracking her gum.

I shuddered.

"I know, right? He didn't find Darlene's EpiPen. Unfortunately, that doesn't seem to bother him. I'm not sure he really even wanted to look for it, to be honest. I think he just wanted to be alone with me."

I shuddered again while Charlie made a face. Hannah gave a knowing nod.

"Men like that shouldn't be in law enforcement, but it seems like there's always a surplus of them."

"So, what do we do now?" Danny asked, his eyes bright. "We're not gonna sit back and let this murder slide, are we?"

I was surprised, given what happened the last time Danny helped us track down a trio of murderers, that he was so gung-ho. The knock he'd taken on the head a few months ago must not have gotten him down too much.

"We don't know that it's murder, though. Deputy Tucker seems pretty convinced it was just an accidental death. Tragic, but not a murder."

"Ha. And we're gonna take his word for it?" Charlie asked, thumbing towards the window where Tucker was wedging himself behind the wheel of his cruiser. "Not likely. What's our next move?"

Ben and Hannah exchanged a smile before Ben looked at me.

"I think we need to pay Ethan a visit. Do you want to come with us?"

Did I? I chewed on my bottom lip until Charlie elbowed me in the side.

"Go on, Eden. It's Sunday and you don't need to be here. Go see Ethan and see what he has to say."

I shot her a glare, but she knew it was toothless and rolled her eyes before sticking out her tongue at me. A tongue dyed bright blue by her gum. It was hard, no impossible, to stay mad at her.

"Sure. Why not?"

I hoped I sounded more confident than I felt. I wasn't sure about seeing Ethan again. It had been a long time. But at least I'd have Hannah and Ben along as backup. Hopefully, their presence would make things less awkward.

"Great," Ben said, smiling, his eyes crinkling up in the corners. "I'll go grab the cats. Meet you two at the Blazer. I'll drive."

Charlie and Wendy heaved twin sighs as Ben walked outside. Danny frowned and straightened.

"You're a lucky woman, Hannah. That's all I gotta say," Wendy said, mooning after Ben. "What a man."

"Yeah. Men like him don't grow on trees. He loves cats, too. He's the total package," Charlie said.

"Hey, I like cats."

Danny was clearly miffed, but Charlie either didn't notice or pretended not to. She busied herself behind the desk before turning to Wendy.

"I think I'll go grab some breakfast and then I'm off for the rest of the day. If you need anything, let me know."

Danny trailed after Charlie, looking a little lost as Wendy shook her head. Hannah leaned close and whispered.

"What's up with the two of them? They're obviously crazy about each other."

"Or just crazy," Wendy muttered.

"I know. They really are a great team. I think they're both scared to ruin their friendship, though. When you live and work in the same place, it can get pretty dicey. I don't blame them for being careful."

"True. I didn't think of that," Hannah said, nodding. "Thanks for keeping me company, Wendy."

"Of course," Wendy said, her curls bobbing as she nodded her head. "I hope I can see your cats again. They're adorable."

I followed Hannah outside and turned my face up to the sun, soaking in the warmth. It was another beautiful day, and I wanted to enjoy Hannah and Ben's company, catching up, not chasing after a potential murderer. Ben appeared, lugging three cat carriers, and we rushed ahead to meet him. He handed us each a cat, and I peeked inside to see who I was carrying.

"Careful," Razzy said. "I'm not a sack of potatoes."

I giggled as we filed over to Hannah's Blazer and got situated. Once we were underway, Hannah gave me the okay to unzip their bags, and the cats clambered out, climbing over my lap in their haste to see out the windows and claim their favorite spots. Rudy hesitated near me and I patted my lap. I must have been sitting in his usual spot. He gently walked onto my lap and curled up, purring softly.

"I hope I didn't make everybody mad last night," he said, turning his little face towards mine. "I didn't mean any harm. I just want what's best for that little kit. She's defenseless."

I smoothed his long fur and shook my head.

"I know that, sweetheart. It needed to be said. Luna already wanted her to stay behind when she went back to the clowder, and now we have even more of a reason to make sure that happens."

Hannah spun around in her seat as Ben drove towards the town of Valewood.

"Do you have someone in mind who could take her? She's going to need a special person."

Razzy's blue eyes blazed as she stared at Hannah with enough force I thought Hannah was going to wince.

"I don't. Not yet. I was thinking maybe someone here at the resort could adopt her. That way Luna can still visit."

Razzy's little shoulders eased and she let out an audible sigh. Gus nuzzled her cheek, whispering to her. Hannah reached back and booped Razzy on the nose.

"Three cats is plenty for us," she said, reassuring her cat. "No one is going to replace you."

Razzy shifted, looking down.

"I'm not trying to be a pain, or heartless," she said, glancing at Rudy. "If the kit needs a home and no one else could take her, I guess she could come live with us."

Hannah and I shared a smile.

"I don't think that will happen," Hannah said. "But I appreciate the offer. You're a great cat, Razz."

The Ragdoll preened under Hannah's praise while Rudy nestled closer to me.

"What happened at the meeting?" Gus asked. "I wish we could have gone with you. I wanted to see if anyone was lying."

I blinked as I looked at him.

"You can tell that?"

"Oh yes," Razzy said, jumping into the conversation. "We can practically smell lies. When people get nervous, the smell of their sweat changes. We're better than lie detectors."

"Yeah, some people get really stinky," Rudy said. "It's kinda gross, but she's right. We can smell lies."

"I didn't know," I said, mystified. "That's so interesting."

"So, did Milton seem shady?" Razzy asked, steering us back to the topic. "I swear there's something wrong with that man."

"I wouldn't say he was shady," Ben said, his tone thoughtful. "Heartless? Yes. Completely disconnected from his wife in life, and even more so in death? Absolutely."

He'd hit the nail on the head. Milton Prescott was not a loving husband, no matter how difficult it might have been to love Darlene. Something had happened to their relationship long before they'd shown up at the resort.

"Interesting. Any good leads?"

"Not much. That Ryan guy, though," Hannah said. "He's a piece of work. So rude. I have questions about Marissa, too. There's something off about her."

I leaned forward, interested.

"What do you mean?"

"I just think it's a little odd that she offered to help someone she doesn't even know arrange his dead wife's funeral. I mean, I get being nice and helpful, but that's taking it a little far."

"Unless they know each other," Razzy said, her voice tight with excitement. "Maybe they're having an affair."

That brought the late night walk I'd witnessed back to my mind. Who had been walking with Milton? Was it innocent? Someone attempting to help a bereaved man? I simply didn't know.

"That seems risky," Ben said. "That would come to light, eventually."

Razzy stomped her white mittened foot.

"Not really. All they'd have to say is they met during the worst of times and bonded while she helped him plan the funeral. No one would be the wiser."

Ben pulled into the parking lot at the police station and I stared at the doors, suddenly feeling shy. What if Ethan didn't want to see me? He hadn't exactly been beating down my door lately. We still texted occasionally, but things had cooled off since the showdown that had nearly ended my life a few months ago.

The cats clambered over me, heading back to their carrying cases, while Hannah shook her head.

"Sorry, Eden. They're not used to having someone in the backseat."

Since they'd distracted me, even for a moment, from worrying about Ethan, I didn't mind. Not one bit.

"They're fine. Are we taking them inside? Ethan doesn't mind cats. He's always been friendly with Jasper and Willow."

"Willow, she's the cute little tortoiseshell in the clowder, right?" Hannah asked. "I'd like to talk more with her."

Razzy's eyes narrowed from her spot in her bag as I zipped up the door. She was a sweet cat, but she was definitely protective of her mama.

"That's her. She's been a tremendous help in a couple of cases. Especially the one where we reunited a little girl with a feral cat she'd fallen in love with. Ethan helped with that one, too."

Ben smiled as he turned off the car and faced me.

"Well, let's get everyone inside and pick his brain. Maybe he'll have some ideas about what we can do to keep this case open."

"I hope so."

We trooped inside, each carrying a bag. If the officer at the front desk had questions about what we were doing, he kept them to himself as he directed us back to Ethan's office. Hannah leaned close as we walked down the hall.

"We lucked out that he's here. I suppose we should've called ahead of time to warn him."

I nodded, unable to answer since nerves had turned my mouth into a near replica of the Sahara desert. Ben rapped on the door bearing Ethan's name and we waited. I heard his voice and my heart gave a little flip.

"Come on in."

It was clear Ethan had not expected to see Ben, Hannah, or me as we got settled into his office. I stowed the cat's bags while Ethan caught up with Ben amidst a little back slapping and a few hand-shakes. It was clear they truly liked one another, and it made me smile to see Ethan so animated. His sky-blue eyes brightened when we made eye contact. At least, I hoped they did, and I wasn't imag-ining things.

"Eden. I've been meaning to call you. How are you?"

I nodded sharply as emotions swirled in my stomach, making me feel nauseous.

"Fine."

He frowned a little, but motioned for everyone to take a seat. He immediately popped back up.

"I'm sorry. Did anyone want anything to drink? We've got dubious coffee or lukewarm water. Take your pick."

Hannah laughed, a rich sound, and shook her head.

"I'm fine. Eden?"

"No, thank you."

Ben leaned back in his chair, crossed his ankle over his knee, and tilted his head to the side.

"How well do you know Deputy Jason Tucker?"

Ethan lowered himself back into his chair, his face alight with curiosity.

"A little. Why?"

"Is he a good cop?"

"Now there's a loaded question if I've ever heard one. What's going on?"

I sat and listened as Hannah and Ben described what had taken place on our hike. Every so often, Ethan's eyes would glance over mine as I added a few things to the conversation. He slowly nodded once we were finished.

"I see. Do you know the coroner's name? I have a few contacts. I could help."

I closed my eyes, trying to recall the name Tessa mentioned. It popped into my mind suddenly.

"Doctor Hastings. Do you know him?"

Ethan smiled and leaned back in his chair.

"As a matter of fact, I do. He was friends with my dead. We shouldn't have any problem getting the autopsy results from him. You're convinced it is murder?"

Ben moved his head from side to side and made a motion with his hand.

"I wouldn't say I'm convinced. Highly suspicious."

"Take me through it one more time," Ethan said, grabbing a pen and a legal pad from behind his desk. "I want to take some notes."

Even though I still felt awkward around him, I was absurdly glad we visited him. Even just talking the case through made me feel better. If there was something to find, Ethan would help us. I was certain of it.

Chapter Thirteen

Even though I'd lived through it and gone over what happened to Darlene Prescott several times, something still didn't feel right. I wasn't sure it was Briar's ominous warning that unsettled me, or that the cats were certain it hadn't been a tragic accident, but I felt driven to find the truth.

Once we'd finished telling Ethan everything, I waited, as though we were in a courtroom, waiting to hear the judge's verdict. Would he agree with us, or was going to dismiss our worries? I inched closer to the edge of my seat. My hopes soared as he nodded.

"I agree. There are a few things that aren't adding up. Let me call Doctor Hastings and see if he's completed the autopsy."

Hannah reached out and gripped my hand, squeezing it as Ethan picked up his desk phone. The seconds seemed to drag on as he was connected with the doctor. I held my breath as he went through a little small talk before getting to the questions about the case.

"Have you finished Darlene Prescott's autopsy?"

Time seemed to stand still, and I wished he'd put the call on speakerphone. I leaned a little closer, but I could only make out the sound of the doctor's voice, not the words he was saying. All we had to go by was the expression on Ethan's face. His forehead wrinkled, and he sat up straighter.

"Really? That's interesting. And you're certain?"

I nearly let out a whimper of frustration as the silence stretched out as he listened to the doctor. Finally, Ethan signed off the call and replaced the handset, his face serious. His eyes met mine before he focused on Ben.

"Darlene Prescott died because of anaphylaxis, due to ingesting shellfish. But there's something odd about the contents of her stomach."

"What?" I asked, unable to stay quiet. "What's odd?"

"He found trace amounts of tropomyosin in her stomach, but there are questions it was enough to cause such a severe allergic reaction. Higher levels were found in her bloodstream, which doesn't add up. He's still running tests."

"What does that mean?" Hannah asked, scooting forward like I had.

"He's seen nothing like this before. He's certain of the cause of death, but the means of delivery are still up in the air. You're certain there was nothing with shellfish in the food? He said that sometimes cross contamination can be responsible for allergic deaths, but from the amount he found in her bloodstream, she would've been exposed to a lot."

"How do we prove it? Can he test the food we had Tessa save?"

"Unfortunately, his role only goes so far, so his hands are tied. At least officially. He recommended we contact the college in Collinsville. They have a lab there that can run the tests. He said he'd help us on his own time."

I wiped my palms on my shorts and nodded.

"Good. We need to call Tessa and get that food to the lab. Is there any risk of the samples degrading?"

"No. As long as they've been kept refrigerated, we should be able to tell. You're certain she wouldn't have thrown them away?"

"I'm positive," I said, nodding. "Tessa and Deputy Tucker don't get along. She agreed with us that there was something strange about the death. I'll call her and double check, though."

I dialed Tessa's number on my cellphone and chewed on my thumbnail while I waited for her to pick up.

"Hi Eden. Have you heard anything about the case?"

"A few things. You've still got that food saved, right?"

"I've got it. You found out something, didn't you?"

I breathed a sigh of relief and shook my head, even though she couldn't see me.

"We still don't think it was accidental. Are you going to be around? Doctor Hastings agreed to have the food tested at the local college lab. We can drive there and pick it up."

"My schedule is clear. In fact, why don't we meet for lunch at Meggie's restaurant? She'd love to meet everyone and I know it would do her a world of good to figure out what was in the food that killed Mrs. Prescott. She's been sick with grief ever since she heard."

"We'll head your way now. What's the name of the restaurant?"

"It's the Robin's Roost. I'll send you a map link. See you soon."

My phone chimed with a text right after I ended the call. I smiled at Hannah.

"She kept the food. We're meeting her for lunch at her friend's restaurant. It's about a forty-five minute drive."

"Great," Hannah said, standing. "We really appreciate your help, Ethan."

He fiddled with a pen on his desk and once again, our eyes met.

"I've got a lunch break coming up. Do you mind if I come with you? I know it's not in my jurisdiction, but I'll admit I'm curious about this."

"The more the merrier," Ben said as he grabbed Gus's bag from under his seat. "I'd appreciate your opinion on it. Do you want to ride with us? We can put the cats in the back of the blazer so there's room."

I heard Razzy's sniff of indignation as Hannah slid her bag out from under the chair. Apparently, they didn't relish the idea of being relegated to the cargo space.

"I'd better take my truck," Ethan said. "If I get called away, I'll need to come back. Eden, would you like to ride with me? We could, um, catch up."

My cheeks felt hot as Hannah smiled at me, her eyes full of secrets and a hint of mischief. If I didn't know better, I'd swear Ben brought up the cramped car conditions on purpose. I realized I'd waited too long and Ethan's eyes were clouding in what looked suspiciously like hurt. I nodded at him.

"Sure. That would be nice."

I wasn't sure how nice it was going to be, but I didn't have the heart to say no. He grabbed his keys from the drawer in front of him and led the way out of his office. I carried Rudy's bag as I trailed behind everyone. I could just make out his whisper as we walked outside.

"He seems nice, Eden. I liked him when we met him during the wedding. You'll be safe."

Physically, I knew there was nowhere safer than with Ethan. It was my heart's safety that was in question.

"I know, Rudy. I'll see you when we get to the restaurant."

"We'll follow you," Hannah said, giving Ethan a cheery wave.

I handed his bag over to Hannah and followed Ethan to his pickup. I crawled into the cab, surprised by how tidy the interior was. I'd only ever seen him in his department vehicle, which was crammed with radios and other devices.

He fired up the engine and gave me an expectant look. It took me a moment to realize he was waiting for directions.

"Oh! Sorry. We can just take the main highway towards Collinsville. The restaurant is just a few streets off the main road."

We pulled out onto the highway and I wished I'd kept Rudy, even though I wasn't sure if Ethan would appreciate cat hair all over the interior of his immaculate truck. Probably not. But it would've been nice to have a furry friend to cling to. I wouldn't have felt so alone. So exposed. The radio was off, and we sat in silence for a few minutes, but they felt like hours.

"How are the clowder cats? Jasper?"

I startled at the sound of his voice and automatically smiled at the thought of the grizzled cat waiting for me back in my cabin.

"Great. They're all thriving, especially in this nice weather. Jasper's doing well. He seems happy. How's work been going?"

"Busy," Ethan said, grimacing, while he shot me a look before focusing back on the road. "I just finished up a brutal case. It took everything we had to solve it. I lost some sleep trying to figure it out."

Part of me wished we were close enough so that I could help him with his cases. I wanted to know more, but I wasn't sure it was my place to ask. I simply nodded and desperately searched for safe conversation.

"I'm glad you figured it out."

He heaved a sigh and glanced in the rearview mirror.

"I'm sorry, you know. I haven't been in touch lately. It wasn't anything you've done. It's just..."

This felt like the old it's not you it's me speech, and I didn't want to hear it. We had a connection. That much was clear. From the first moment we'd met, something had sparked between us. I was drawn to his honest blue eyes, his gentle manner. We'd had a few misunderstandings, but that bond between us was always there. At least, I thought it was. Maybe I'd been wrong about everything.

"You're fine. You don't owe me anything."

I tried to sound natural. Like it didn't matter. But it did. It mattered a lot. Not hearing from him was like a knife in the chest.

"That's not true," Ethan said, his voice soft. "I'm still trying to find balance. I don't expect you to understand. It's not even a good excuse. My job... Well, it takes over my life sometimes. I'm trying to be better. I went so long without talking to you it felt awkward reaching out. I didn't know if maybe you'd... Found someone else. I didn't want to intrude."

"I get that you're busy. I am too. I'm trying to work on my degree, learn an entirely new job, be there for my friends, and take care of the cats. It's a lot sometimes. But I always try to be there for the people who matter."

I blinked, surprised by what came out of my mouth. I hadn't quite intended to say it, but my words were out now, floating around the interior of the pickup. I couldn't take them back. What was even more surprising was I didn't want to. In fact, I felt better having said them.

Ethan's face was drawn as he nodded slowly.

"You're right. That's one of the many things I admire about you."

I tried to lighten the mood.

"That I'm always right?"

He snorted and shot me a look, his expression playful.

"Let's not go too far. No. I admire the fact that you give so much of yourself. I envy that. I've always kept my feelings close to the chest."

I looked out the window at the mountains whizzing past and realized how little I knew about Ethan Rhodes. We'd always been thrown together by murders, and never took much time to know each other outside of the depths of the case. I liked the man. I liked him a lot. But I didn't know him. Not really. He'd done background research on me during the first case we'd worked on together, but he didn't really know me either. Maybe it was time for that to change.

"Do you have any siblings?"

If he was thrown by my conversational shift, he didn't show it. His shoulders relaxed as he recognized the metaphorical olive branch I was offering and grasped it.

"Nope. I was an only child. How about you?"

I settled back in my seat and got to know Ethan. The man, not the detective. The Prescott case still swirled underneath the surface, but for the next twenty minutes, I wanted to focus on this. On us.

Chapter Fourteen

The voice on the GPS app on my phone interrupted Ethan's hilarious retelling of his first time going fishing, and it was a good thing it did, or I would've completely missed the turn. He followed the directions while I wheezed with laughter, my sides aching.

"You flipped the boat over?"

Ethan nodded before giving me a rueful smile.

"Yeah. Luckily, my dad thought it was hilarious. He still tells that story whenever we have family gatherings. I don't think I'll ever live it down."

"But you caught the fish?"

"I caught the fish. I still don't know how it stayed on my line."

"Can you imagine what the fish was thinking?"

That sent us off into more gales of laughter as Ethan pulled into the parking lot of the Robin's Roost. He turned off the truck while I wiped my eyes. It felt good to laugh, and even better to share this moment with him.

"Hannah and Ben should be here soon," he said, pivoting in his seat so he could look at me straight on. "We should go fishing one of these days. There's a cool lake around here, actually. It's pretty quiet."

"That would be fun. I haven't gone fishing since my grandpa was alive. He used to take me out, just me, not my sister. She didn't enjoy fishing. It was our special time, away from my folks. I miss him."

Ethan tilted his head to the side, leaning it against the headrest.

"You don't like to talk about your parents, do you?"

I stared down at my hands and shook my head. My former life was something I didn't like to think about, let alone discuss. It had been an odd childhood, but there were bright moments. Like going fishing with my grandpa. I could almost feel the sun on my face and smell the muddy pond we used to go to.

"No. Not really. Sometimes I miss my sister."

He opened his mouth to say something, but a horn beeped behind us as Hannah and Ben pulled in next to Ethan's truck. I shook off the memories of the past and waved as Hannah hopped out.

"Sorry, we took a wrong turn," Hannah said as we got out of the truck. "Stupid GPS. I should know better than to listen to it."

"Or maybe not toggle the avoid highways button," Ben said, winking at her. "That's always good, too."

She rolled her eyes and looped her arm through mine, glancing back into the car where the three cats were staring back at her. Razzy looked less than pleased.

"I promise. I'll bring back some treats for you guys."

"Hey, everyone," Tessa called out from the front door of the Robin's Roost. "There's a patio out back. Bring the cats along. I've got Finn and Briar with me."

The cats lit up, and Ethan laughed as he saw their expressions.

"I'd swear they understood what she was saying right then. Look at their eyes."

"Cats are extremely intelligent," Hannah said, exchanging a quick glance with me. "You'd be surprised at how much they understand."

A soft woof sounded, and I turned to see Finn walking towards us, her white-tipped tail waving like a flag. Ethan immediately brightened and held out a hand while Hannah and Ben loaded the cats into their bags for the brief trip.

"This is Finn," I said, reaching down to scratch behind Finn's ears. "She was with us on the hike. I don't see Briar. She must be out back."

Ethan was obviously taken with the beautiful border collie.

"What a wonderful dog."

Tessa motioned for us to follow her around the side of the wooden building, and we followed a paver path back to an area that could only be described as magical. Several tables were arranged under a wooden overhang. Quirky chairs circled them, their cushions brightly colored, inviting people to sit and relax. I immediately liked the place, but admittedly, the amazing smells coming from the kitchen played a big role in that, too.

"This is great," Hannah said, offloading Razzy's bag onto the ground. "Guys, I'm going to keep your harnesses on, but best behavior, okay?"

She let the cats out one by one as Ethan continued lavishing attention on Finn. The dog leaned over and gave me a quick lick on the hand before focusing back on Ethan. Tessa watched their interaction, and I realized I'd neglected to introduce them.

"Tessa, this is Ethan Rhodes. He's a detective back in Valewood. Ethan, this is Tessa Windsor, the owner of Wild Peak Expeditions. Finn's her dog."

Ethan tore himself away from the dog long enough to shake Tessa's hand.

"Nice to meet you. I've heard good things about your company. I think a few of my friends have gone on some of your night hikes."

"Ooh, night hikes? How cool would that be?" Hannah asked, her eyes shining.

"They're great," Tessa said, nodding. "My favorite is the Milky Way hike I do in the late summer. It's magical."

"We'll have to come back and do that," Ben said, smiling as he took Hannah's hand. "That sounds like a great way to see the stars."

I sat down, sinking into the comfortable cushion, as Briar

strolled out of the restaurant. Her beautiful coat shone under the sunlight as she strolled in our direction. She took a seat in front of Ethan, studying him. He chuckled and reached a hand down for her to smell. She sniffed delicately before nodding once. Apparently, he'd passed her inspection.

A tall woman came out of the cafe, her ruddy face split in a smile. Her curly black hair was corralled in a high ponytail, but her vibrantly blue eyes were the first thing I noticed.

"This is Meggie Dolan, the owner of the restaurant. Meggie, meet everyone."

"Hi, everyone," Meggie said, shaking her head at Tessa. "Names are always nice. It's good to meet all of you. I've heard nothing but good things."

Hannah leaned forward and shook Meggie's hand.

"That's a relief. I'm Hannah and this is Ben. You have a beautiful place here. Very eclectic, but also very zen. I love it."

Meggie lit up and nodded, her curls bouncing.

"That's exactly what I was going for. Nice to meet you. And you must be Eden?"

I shook her hand and nodded towards Ethan.

"I am. Nice to meet you. This is Ethan Rhodes."

"Well, now that we're old friends, I hope everyone's hungry. We've got green chile burgers on special today."

Hannah's hand shot up, and she nodded.

"One for me, please!"

"Better make that two," Ben said with a chuckle.

Ethan looked at me, and I nodded.

"Two more of the same. Whatever you're making in there, it smells delicious."

Meggie dimpled and turned towards Tessa, who made a swirling motion with her finger.

"Green chile burgers all around. Like I could ever turn one of those down. I'm telling you, guys, you gotta dip the curly fries in the sauce. Incredible. And I'm not just saying that because Meggie and I have been friends since third grade."

Meggie swatted her and disappeared back into the cafe. I looked around the peaceful patio and sighed. I hadn't expected to enjoy myself, given what we were investigating, but there was something special about being surrounded by friends.

"So, what did you find out?" Tessa asked, stroking the silky fur on Finn's ears. "I still can't get over how she died."

I glanced at Hannah, who gave me a friendly nod.

"She died after suffering a severe allergic reaction to a compound found in shellfish."

"What?! Shellfish? That's not possible."

Ethan scooted closer to the table.

"You're certain? It might have been an ingredient in a side dish. Eden mentioned there was a potato salad. Any chance it might have had crab or shrimp in it?"

"Not a chance. When the lady at the resort, sorry, I can't remember her name, but when she called and read me the list of Mrs. Prescott's allergies, I was certain that shellfish was the least of our worries. Meggie would never use that in anything she prepared. She's allergic to it as well. I still remember when we were kids when she found out about that allergy. Her parents grilled up some surf and turf. It was terrible. They barely got her to the hospital in time. Actually, it was really similar to what happened to Darlene. I can't believe I forgot that."

"What about the food you bought separately? Is there a chance it could have been in there? Even cross contamination?"

"I don't think so, but the labels are right on the food containers. The only thing I bought special for her were the chips and the corn salad. We can check the labels, but I wouldn't think that shellfish would be in there."

Meggie came back out, carrying a tray with our drinks. Her steps slowed when she saw the looks on our faces.

"What?"

"Darlene Prescott was killed by a shellfish allergen," Tessa said. "Just like the one you have. I was just explaining why it wasn't possible that the food you made was contaminated."

Meggie slid the tray onto the table and sank down into an empty seat, her face pale.

"Oh my goodness. That's terrible. It's such an awful feeling when your throat closes like that. I can't even kiss someone who's eaten shellfish. It's that severe. That poor woman. Where was her EpiPen? I always have mine on me."

"We need to check the containers on the other food," Ben said, frowning.

"Let's do it right now," Meggie said, jumping back up, wringing her hands. "The food is right in the walk-in, in the totes Tessa brought yesterday."

We all jumped up, dislodging cats, and Finn barked sharply, her eyes never leaving Tessa's face.

"Well, maybe not all of us," Ethan said, smiling to break the tension. "I'll go look. I'm not involved in the case, and that's probably smart. Meggie, if you could show me?"

"Sure, come this way."

We sank back into our seats and the cats slunk back out from under the table. Rudy patted my leg with his paw and I motioned to my lap. He jumped up and sat, staring across at Hannah. I knew how hard it must be for them to want to speak, and I wished they could. Heck, they could probably examine the food and determine if it was contaminated.

"So, if it's not in the food, how did she ingest it?" Tessa said, crossing her arms over her chest and rubbing her biceps. "It makes little sense."

"If it's not in the food, then somehow, someone must have slipped her something that contained the allergen. Which means it's murder. That's what we're afraid of. If Deputy Tucker doesn't agree, someone could get away with murder."

"We can't let that happen," Tessa said, her voice sharp, making Finn woof softly at her side. "We just can't. Jace isn't a corrupt cop, no matter what I think of him as a person. If we can find proof, he'll listen to us."

Ben leaned back in his chair, his expression clearly doubting that statement.

"You're certain?"

"Positive. If he doesn't, my brother, Paul, owns the newspaper in town. We can turn up the heat until he pays attention."

Her grin was positively feral, and I liked her even more. Tessa was just as motivated to find justice as we were. Ethan rejoined us on the patio, shaking his head.

"Nothing on the labels. We'll take the food to the lab after we eat. If something is in there, it was definitely added after it was made."

We began tossing around ideas as Rudy shifted on my lap. I stroked his soft fur, and he leaned back into me. I'd have to wait to get the cat's opinions, and I was certain they had a few ideas. Whoever had killed Darlene Prescott wouldn't get away with it. Not if we had anything to say about it.

Chapter Fifteen

After a delicious lunch that guaranteed I'd be coming back to the Robin's Roost regularly, we said our goodbyes, grabbed the tote full of food, and headed out to the lab. Once again, I rode with Ethan, but this time, I felt much more at ease. The former awkwardness was gone, and we found plenty of things to talk about. We passed a lake, filled with boats and people paddle boarding, enjoying the bright sunshine, and for a moment, I wished I was out there, blind to the ugliness I'd witnessed the day before.

"That's a fun lake," Ethan said, smiling. "Maybe sometime we could rent some paddle boards and try it."

"I'd like that."

We pulled into the university lab and found a place to park. I spotted the county coroner's van and breathed a sigh of relief. He was here and soon, he'd help us figure out just how Darlene had been killed. Ben and Hannah pulled in next to us while Ethan got out and took the tote out of his truck's backseat. His phone rang, and he frowned while he fished it out of his pocket. He walked away a few steps and took the call. I watched as his shoulders tensed and Hannah nudged me with her elbow.

"It's an official call. I'd know that look anywhere. That's what used to happen with Ben and me until he left the department. That's probably the thing I miss the least."

Ethan ended the call, stowed his phone, and walked back, grimacing.

"I've got to go. It's pretty urgent."

"I'll take this in," Ben said, reaching for the handles of the tote. "It's probably best if you don't get involved too much, given that it's Tucker's case."

Ethan frowned again, but nodded, and agreed to call Doctor Hastings and let him know Ben would meet him. He turned to me, hand on his phone.

"I'm sorry, Eden. I was hoping to take you back to the resort. Maybe we can catch up soon? It was good to see you again, Hannah. Hopefully, you and Ben can stop by before you leave."

I nodded as he got in his pickup and headed out. Once his pickup disappeared, I turned to Hannah.

"What are the cats thinking? It was killing me not being able to ask them about their theories."

Hannah gave me a long look before she answered.

"You'll know when the time is right."

"What?"

"Whether to tell Ethan about the cat thing. You'll know. If I can give you some advice, make certain of him before you do. It's difficult. I remember when I told Ben. He said some pretty mean things and took off. It wasn't until much later that he finally believed me. Now, we're lucky enough to share this gift, but that doesn't mean it was easy at first. Give it time, Eden. If he's the right one, it will all fall into place."

I nodded, unable to speak around the lump in my throat. Somehow, she'd known exactly what I was thinking. She wrapped me in a hug and patted my back. At least I had my friends. Charlie knew about my secret and she hadn't judged me. Hannah was right. The right people wouldn't.

She pulled back and opened the back door of the Blazer, revealing three sets of curious eyes. Razzy blinked slowly at me as

Rudy nuzzled my hand. Gus dipped his tipped ears in my direction and spoke, bringing tears to my eyes.

"You deserve the best, Eden. Never forget that."

"So, what do you guys think? Was it the food or did someone slip her something?" Hannah asked once I'd recovered.

"We've been talking about it," Razzy said. "There was something odd that happened right after we got to the trailhead. Do you remember? The drive wasn't that long, but Marissa disappeared into the restrooms and took forever."

I blushed and shrugged.

"Maybe something didn't agree with her. We humans aren't as good at controlling our bodily functions as you guys are."

"I still think it was odd. Briar mentioned something before we even got to the lake. She said Finn sensed something was wrong. The food was already delivered to the campsite, so it's not like she would've sensed something. It's not adding up."

I nodded slowly, closing my eyes as I took myself back to the first hour of our hike. Briar had told me much the same thing. How had she known? How had Finn known?

"You're right. And we're still dealing with the missing Epipen. Wait," I said as I straightened up, and looked at Hannah, grabbing for her arm. "Hear me out. What if Darlene had her EpiPen with her when we left the resort, but someone took it out of her purse and stashed it in the restroom? I know it sounds crazy, but..."

"I don't think that's crazy at all," Razzy said, excitement clear in her voice. "Where was Marissa sitting?"

"A row back from Darlene. I remember because Darlene made a big fuss about wanting the best seat. It's a bus, the seats are all the same. She was right behind them. But how would she do that without Darlene noticing?"

I screwed up my lips, frustrated. Suddenly, Gus's deep voice sounded, forcing me back to the present.

"What if Milton took the EpiPen and handed it to Marissa? What if they're working together? That makes more sense."

Hannah's eyebrows went up, and she nodded.

"You're right, Gus."

The door to the lab swung open, revealing Ben. He walked towards us, his hands buried deeply in his pockets, shoulders slumped. Hannah went to him, drawn like a moth to a flame.

"Honey, what's wrong?"

His face cleared, and he shrugged.

"Nothing's wrong. The doctor was very nice, but he said it would take at least a few days to run all the tests. We may not know until next week."

And by then they'd be back in Golden Hills, away from the action. I completely understood the way he was feeling.

"Ben, we've got a lead that will cheer you up," Razzy said, bounding out of the Blazer and striding over to him, tail held confidently. "We need to go back to the trailhead and check out the restroom."

For a moment, Ben looked confused, but Razzy's excitement was infectious. Hannah nodded while Rudy joined Razzy, nimbly hopping over her back, much to her displeasure.

"Come on! We're on to something fantastic!"

Ben shared a smile and looked around.

"Where's Ethan?"

"He got called back to Valewood. I hope you don't mind if I tag along with you two."

Hannah laughed as she took Ben's hand and led him over to the car.

"It would be a long walk, otherwise. Of course not, silly. Hop in. Let's go investigate a restroom. Oh gosh, that's a sentence I never thought I'd say."

We all got back into the Blazer, and once again, Rudy hopped into my lap, his purr making his sides vibrate. He stayed perched on my lap, staring out the window as we drove back to the trailhead. Finally, he turned to me, his eyes serious.

"Have you figured out what to do with the girl kitten yet?"

I hadn't. In fact, it had almost completely slipped my mind. She was going to need a very special home, one where her disability wouldn't be a liability. Everyone I knew at the resort was busy with work, and Charlie already had one cat. I didn't think Benny was the type of cat to enjoy a roommate.

"I don't know, Rudy. I want what's best for her. Like you said, she's special, and she deserves a loving home."

Gus let out a rumble, deep in his chest, and I met his green eyes. His tail twitched as he looked at me.

"If you ask me, she grew up in a loving home. That's all she's ever known. Why change it? In fact, she'd probably be more comfortable staying in the place where she was raised. The kits will begin talking soon. Maybe you can ask her."

I blinked, stunned by the beautiful simplicity of Gus's words. He was right. She'd already spent the first two months of her life with me. Jasper had grown used to sharing the cabin with Luna and her litter. It had given him life, that little extra pep in his step. Maybe a young kitten would be just what he needed. I nodded.

"I'll ask Jasper what he thinks. It was his home first. If he doesn't mind sharing, I'd love to keep her."

"See, problem solved," Hannah said, clapping in the front seat. "I can't think of anyone better for that little kitten than you, Eden. She'd thrive with you."

Ben pulled off the road, into the empty trailhead, and parked. I had a potential plan for the kitten, but we still had a mystery to solve. I stared at the low slung restrooms. If I was desperate to hide something in there, where would it be?

"Let's see what we can find. We'll take the ladies' room, Ben. Check the other one, just in case. She was gone for a while."

"We're coming too," Razzy announced, from her spot on Hannah's lap. "You need our superior senses."

I wouldn't turn down their help, that's for sure. If there was one thing I'd learned about cats, it was they were nearly as talented as bloodhounds with finding things. We got out, and the boys split off with Ben to search the men's room. Hannah pushed open the door, allowing Razzy to go in first. I followed on their heels. The door thumped closed behind me, making me jump.

Hannah turned around slowly.

"Oh, wow. This is nice. Not at all what I expected."

She was right. The restrooms looked reasonably new. The long sink dominated one side of the room, and in the center, there was a space for a trash can. Hannah and I glanced at each other.

"Who wants to dig through the trash?"

Razzy heaved a sigh and hopped on the counter, sniffing around the edge of the container.

"It doesn't smell awful," she said, but her tone let me know it didn't smell great, either.

"I'll take it," Hannah said, joining Razzy and peering down into the can's depths. "It hasn't been emptied recently, which I guess is a good thing."

That left me with the stalls. There were three of them, all behind metal doors. I walked into the first one and looked around. A small waste can was next to the toilet, and there was a plastic toilet paper dispenser. I steeled myself and peeked inside the can. Empty. The toilet paper holder was next, but it had nothing to hide. I looked at the toilet. What if she'd flushed the Epipen? I hadn't even considered that. If she had, we would likely never know, unless they could order the septic tank to be emptied. I shuddered. Now there was a job I wouldn't want to do.

I went into the other two stalls while Hannah put her hand into the trash can as far as it would go, her face pulled into a disgusted expression. Once I'd confirmed the waste cans were empty, I came back out and looked into the small mirror over the sinks, meeting Hannah's eyes.

"Nothing, huh? We came up empty, too."

"Do you think she flushed it?"

Hannah slid off the counter and shrugged.

"If she'd been smart, she would have."

"Do you think she is, though?" Razzy asked. "She was here forever. She took the time to hide it, not dispose of it. Besides, aren't they worth a lot of money? Maybe she intended to come back and sell it on the black market."

Hannah brightened.

"Did you check the tanks? Do these toilets have the lids on the back that come off? Maybe you're right, Razzy."

The three of us crowded into the first stall. Razzy's nose wrinkled as I carefully took off the lid and peered down into the tank. Nothing.

"Let's check on the others."

I put the lid back while Hannah hurried into the next stall. The grinding sound of porcelain was followed by a shout of victory.

"Aha! We've got it! Ben!"

Her voice echoed through the small space, and seconds later, Ben stuck his head through the door.

"Yes, my love?"

"Do you still carry gloves in your pocket?"

"Always. Did you find it?"

"We did! It's been in water, so I doubt there will be any prints, but we can definitely place Marissa at the scene."

Ben's eyes were bright with excitement as he pulled on a pair of disposable gloves and joined Hannah in the stall. I watched from the stall's doorway as he carefully fished the small Epipen out of the tank and held it up. I let out a long breath. We'd found the smoking gun. Now, all we needed to do was get Marissa to admit her guilt.

A scratching sound at the door grabbed my attention and I quickly let Gus and Rudy in so they could join in the celebration. I'd never thought I'd be excited about finding an Epipen in a bathroom, but here we were. Hannah took a baggie out of her purse and Ben slid the medication inside before removing his gloves.

"We need to get this to Deputy Tucker right away."

I nodded, and we streamed back outside. It meant another detour to Collinsville, but that was just fine. We were that much closer to building the case. Our suspicions were right. Now, we just needed the last pieces to prove it.

Chapter Sixteen

Ben drew the metaphorical short straw and called Deputy Tucker as we drove back to Collinsville. We had the smoking gun, but it wouldn't do us any good if we couldn't convince Tucker to hear us out. Well, unless we could somehow do a citizen's arrest and I wasn't entirely sure how that would work, and highly doubted Marissa and Milton would go along with it. I tapped my fingers on my knees as I listened to Ben's half of the conversation.

"Yes, I know this is your case, but we literally just found Darlene Prescott's EpiPen."

Another pause that felt entirely too long filled the vehicle with silence. I sure hope Ben didn't mind that there were five sets of ears listening in. Razzy's eyes were narrowed to mere slits from her spot on Hannah's lap and I could tell it was taking all of her patience not to say something.

"No, there wasn't a label on it, but don't you think it's pretty strange that there was an EpiPen in the trailhead's restroom, and Darlene's wasn't in her bag?"

Hannah began chewing on her thumbnail and I was tempted to gnaw on mine as we waited again. Ben's face cleared and hope flared brightly in my chest.

"Alright. We'll be there in ten."

Ben ended the call and let out a gusty sigh. All three cats began talking at once and I watched as his lip curled into a half smile as he patiently waited for the cacophony to die down.

"He's not happy about it, but he agreed to meet with us. I don't blame him. It makes him look bad, but at least he's not discounting what we found."

"Yet."

Razzy's dry statement made Hannah chuckle, and I shook my head.

"He can't ignore it, right? I mean, it's got to be hers."

"No, it's a big enough find to at least cast doubt on Marissa and Milton. I wish we could get Ethan to run them both, to see if they know each other. They had to be working together. This isn't just a spur-of-the-moment crime."

"She offered to help organize Darlene's funeral, remember? How awful is that if she's the one who helped kill her?" I asked.

"It was definitely premeditated," Gus said. "I wonder how long they've had this planned. If you hadn't thought to check the restroom, Razzy, they might have gotten away with it."

Razzy preened on the front seat while Rudy shifted on my lap. From my conversations with Hannah, I knew the cats had a friendly rivalry about who was the better investigator. I stroked his back and planted a kiss between his ears.

"We're all in this together, Rudy."

He turned, eyes bright, and blinked slowly. He really was the sweetest cat. Hannah pulled up directions to the sheriff's office in Collinsville and within minutes, we were parked in the lot. The beige brick building nearly blended into the surrounding scenery. Ben took the keys out, gave them to Hannah, and put his hand on the door.

"I'd better go in alone."

"What?!"

Razzy stomped her mittened foot on Hannah's leg and stared at Ben, who gave her a sheepish smile.

"It's going to be hard enough to convince Tucker to do what we want. Now, imagine all of us trooping in with our menagerie and demanding the same thing."

"It's not fair."

Hannah stroked Razzy's back.

"I know, sweetheart. Humans rarely are fair."

"I'm sorry," Ben said, chucking Razzy under the chin. "We wouldn't be able to do this without you."

She nodded and Ben leaned over, kissed Hannah on the cheek, and gave Razzy a quick peck before heading into the building. My stomach clenched into knots. Now, we just needed to wait. Would Tucker agree with us?

"I just thought of something," Hannah said, sitting bolt upright, much to Razzy's displeasure. "We need to make sure they don't leave the resort. I mean, I know they can't hide forever, but if they're gone, it's going to make it even harder to catch them."

"I'm on it," I said, grabbing for my phone. "I'll ask Trevor to keep them there."

I punched in Trevor's number and waited, drumming my fingers again. I felt like I needed to race back to the resort and tackle them myself. Trevor came on the line.

"Eden? What's wrong?"

"I can't explain right this instant, but can you make sure two guests don't check out? Milton Prescott and Marissa... Oh shoot, I don't know her last name."

I had to give Trevor credit. He didn't hesitate or ask questions.

"I'll find it. She's part of the wildflower tour package?"

"Yep. Thanks, Trevor. I'll fill you in as soon as we get back."

"You're not here?"

"I'm in Collinsville with Hannah and Ben. We're at the sheriff's office."

"Well, now I'm really intrigued. I'll let Wendy know and I'll post Josh at the door. I'll rope Danny in to watch the other exit."

"Great. We'll be back soon. I appreciate it, Trevor."

I signed off and let out a sigh of relief.

"He's going to do it."

"He's a good guy. I never got to meet his wife, but I heard she's a character."

I smiled, remembering the last time I'd seen the tiny Annie next to her bear of a husband.

"She's a firecracker. They're well suited."

"Tell me more about Danny and Charlie," Hannah said, leaning against the passenger seat. "Since we're talking about characters."

I spent the next ten minutes regaling her with stories about my friends at the resort and the adventures we'd experienced. I'd told her some of it before, but it was a great distraction. The cats loved hearing about how Willow and I had helped reunite Charity and Dex. We were so deep in conversation, Ben startled us when he opened the door.

He gave us a triumphant smile as he slid into the driver's seat.

"He agreed with us. He'll meet us back at the resort."

"Is he going to arrest them?"

"He's definitely going to question them. He's got to do this the right way. You know how it works."

"Hmmph," Razzy said, sniffing. "They'd better not try to wiggle out of this. They're guilty. I know it."

Ben fired up the Blazer, and we began the trek back to the resort. We'd driven this road more times in the past two days than I had since I'd moved to the resort, but I still looked out at the surrounding mountains with a feeling of awe. Maybe someday I'd climb to the top of one of them. I'd never even attempted a four-teen-er, but Charlie had. She'd been trying to persuade me to do it with her and right now, I was tempted to accept. What would the view be like from the tallest peaks?

I turned to see Gus watching me, his eyes keen on my face. I wasn't sure if mind-reading was one of his gifts, but I wouldn't put it past him. He was a remarkable cat, quiet, at least compared to Razzy and Rudy, but when he spoke, it was always measured and thoughtful. I smiled as he shifted his giant paws on the backseat.

"What are you thinking about, Gus?"

"I'm happy we came up to see you."

"Me too."

Simple words, but they meant more than he could have guessed. Rudy snuggled into my chest as we got closer to the resort. I missed Jasper and wished he could have gone with us. He hadn't left the cabin often, not since the kittens arrived, and I needed to make sure he got out more often. So far, he'd seemed to enjoy his time living inside, but I wanted to make sure he kept enjoying it.

We pulled onto the highway that led to the resort, and Hannah turned in her seat again.

"Do you remember what car Milton drove? How about Marissa?"

I shook my head.

"No. We don't collect that information when guests check in. Maybe we should."

"Hmm. No worries. I was thinking we could make sure they were still there and put out an APB if they left."

"Good idea, lady," Gus said, nodding his approval. "Aren't there cameras at the entrance? There were the last time we were here."

I perked up and nodded.

"There are. Trevor can get that information for us. Hopefully it won't come to that."

Ben pulled into the parking lot of the resort and we piled out, the cats close behind. Hannah tilted her head to the side, and Razzy sighed.

"Fine. We'll wait for our bags. I don't know why we can't walk around on our leads. Dogs do it all the time."

I thought back to the snowmobile event when I'd nearly been flattened by someone rushing past on a sled and shook my head.

"It's just too dangerous, sweetie. People speed through the lot, even though they know they shouldn't. It's safer to have you guys in your carriers."

Hannah shot me a grateful look as we got everyone in their bags. I grabbed Rudy's bag and headed for the front door of the resort. I spotted Josh right away as we got closer. He waved as we walked up.

"Hey, Eden. Those two guests haven't been past me since you called. Trevor's got all the exits covered."

"That's great. Do you know if they're still in their rooms?"

"I don't. We didn't want to tip anyone off."

"Good thinking. Deputy Tucker should arrive soon. We'll wait for him."

Josh gave me a friendly nod and shot me a thumbs up before leaning back against the wall. Wendy was talking to a guest at the front desk, so I led everyone back to my office. If nothing else, it would be a good place to stash the cat's bags until we figured out our next move. We'd just walked past Marsburg's office when he popped his head out and smiled.

"Hey, Eden. Hannah and Ben. What's going on? Trevor filled me in, but he said you'd be telling us more when you got back."

I handed Rudy's bag to Hannah and quickly brought my boss up to speed. His expression turned serious as I explained how we'd found the EpiPen.

"I didn't expect that. I figured it was just a tragic accident. You're certain?"

I nodded as Ben and Hannah rejoined us.

"Positive. We still need to figure out how the shellfish got into the meal, but we have enough to question them on why the pen was stolen and hidden."

"Alright. Keep me informed. Let me know when the Deputy arrives. I'll sign off on whatever search he needs."

As we walked back to the front desk, Hannah elbowed me gently.

"I like your office. You've got a pleasant view of the resort."

"I like it too. It's strange having an office, but I've gotten used to it. I need to decorate it a little more. Oh, where are the cats? Did you leave them back there?"

Hannah and Ben exchanged a glance, filled to the brim with a mix of chagrin and humor.

"Just temporarily. We wouldn't dare leave them out of the excitement. We'd never hear the end," Ben said, smiling. "Besides, they needed a break. They may be our little investigators, but they're still cats. As little as they like to admit it, all three of them needed a nap."

Wendy was just finishing up helping the guest at the front as we walked out of the hallway. She shot us a smile and tapped a little on her computer.

"There. Done. Okay, Eden. What's going on? Trevor's ordered someone to man every door and let me know not to let Mr. Prescott or Marissa Whitmore check out, but I'm not sure how I'm going to do that if they show up."

"Whitmore. I didn't know her last name," I said. "Anyway, we found some evidence that links Marissa to the missing EpiPen."

"No way!"

"Do you know if they're still in their rooms?"

"I guess so. I haven't seen them and we haven't checked to make sure. I guess I could see if Penny will send one of her girls up there to ask if they need any towels or something."

I grimaced and shook my head. The less we had to involve Penny, the better.

"No, that's okay. Hopefully, the deputy gets here soon. He was going to be right behind us, wasn't he?"

I turned to Ben, who shrugged and leaned against the desk.

"Let's hope so. Legally, there's only so much we can do to hold them here until he arrives."

"I just hope we're not guarding the hen house only to find out the hens have already left the coop," Wendy said. "You've got to think they'd be wary of being caught. If they're guilty, anyway."

"As far as they know, they've gotten away with murder."

I sobered as Ben spoke. It was all too easy to get caught up in the excitement of finding a major clue, while forgetting we were trying to catch two murderers. If we were right, Darlene Prescott was dead because of these two people. They'd killed once. What was to stop them from killing again?

A squad car rolled past the front windows, and Hannah let out a sigh.

"Finally. I'll go grab the cats."

"I'll help."

We headed back down the hallway and I poked my head into Marsburg's office to let him know what was going on. Hannah reappeared, laden down with two bags, and I darted after her to get the third. If my boss wondered what we were doing, he held his tongue as he followed us back to the front. Just as we walked up to the front desk. Deputy Tucker walked in, heading straight for us. It was time.

Chapter Seventeen

Deputy Tucker hitched up his duty belt as he approached. The radio on his shoulder crackled to life, but he ignored whatever it was saying. He zeroed in on Mr. Marsburg as he came out of the hallway after us.

"You're the owner, right?"

"Yes, sir," Marsburg said, thrusting out his hand for the deputy to shake. "James Marsburg. We set up security at all the exits to make sure neither party left until you got here."

"Nice. Good thinking."

"I can't take credit for it. It was Eden's idea."

I wasn't sure I liked the gleam in Tucker's eyes as he looked at me, and focused my attention on my feet, and the cat carrier sitting next to them. I could almost feel the moment he looked away. My boss came closer, standing behind me almost protectively. It made me feel a smidgen better.

"Alright, so here's what we're gonna do. Miss, if you could call their rooms and have them come down, I'd appreciate it."

Wendy flushed under Tucker's attention and nodded, reaching for the desk phone.

"What should I say?"

"Just that their presence has been requested."

Her fingers shook a little as she dialed the Prescott's room. It seemed to ring forever, but as soon as I saw Wendy straighten, I knew Milton had answered.

"Mr. Prescott? This is Wendy at the front desk. Could you come down for a second? Thank you."

"One down, one to go," Hannah said as she leaned closer to me.

Wendy dialed Marissa's room, and we all waited as the line rang. And rang. She wasn't picking up.

"What do I do?" Wendy asked, looking at the deputy.

"Try again."

She did, but once again, no one picked up the line. I chewed on my bottom lip. Was she with Milton in his room and that's why she didn't answer her phone? Had she already left and made her escape?

The elevator dinged and I could hear it descend. Milton was on his way. Tucker shifted his belt again and cleared his throat.

"We'll deal with Prescott first. Keep trying her."

If Milton wondered why there was a crowd of people and Deputy Tucker standing at the front desk, he hid it well. He smiled broadly at all of us and stuffed his hands in his pockets.

"Yes? Was there something you needed? You already let me know my wife's body was being released."

"Fresh evidence was discovered," Deputy Tucker said, his tone ringing with officialness and officiousness at the same time. "I'd like to ask you some questions."

"Really? That's odd. What's wrong?"

I'd never pegged Milton Prescott as a cool cucumber, but he seemed entirely unconcerned. Were we completely wrong that he'd been involved?

"An EpiPen was discovered in the restroom at the trailhead. We believe it belonged to your wife."

I couldn't help but notice Tucker made it seem like he'd been the one who'd found the EpiPen, but I held my tongue. I was too busy watching Milton to gauge his reaction.

"What's this?"

Wendy spoke into the phone and I realized she must have gotten through to Marissa's room. A jolt went through me as she hung up the phone and nodded at me. I wasn't sure if Tucker had heard.

"Do you recognize this?" Tucker said, holding up the baggie.

"Well, it looks like a tube. Is that what an EpiPen looks like?"

I tilted my head to the side as the elevator headed back upstairs. Marissa would join us shortly. Would she be as unconcerned as Milton?

"Your wife was the one who carried it around with her. I was hoping you could tell me."

"Well, I never dealt with anything like that," Milton said, flashing a smile. "I'm afraid I know nothing about it. Maybe it belonged to someone else."

The elevator doors dinged and released Marissa. She started forward, but her steps ground to a halt as soon as she saw everyone standing around. She pasted on a smile and walked forward, her steps hesitant.

"What's going on? Why did you need me to come down?"

I couldn't help but be impressed at how unconcerned she seemed. The only thing that had betrayed her was that slight hesitation as she left the elevator. I doubted everything we'd learned so far. Were we wrong? Had Darlene truly had an accidental allergy attack, and we were stirring up trouble for nothing? I shook off the doubts. We had the pen. We had the evidence the coroner found in Darlene's system. We were right. We just needed to prove it.

"Miss Whitmore, you were observed going into the restroom at the trailhead before the hike, correct?"

She flushed a dark red and nodded.

"Yes, that's true. I'm afraid I don't understand why that's relevant."

Once again, Tucker held up the baggie.

"This was found in that restroom and is believed to have belonged to Mrs. Prescott. Do you have anything to say about why this was found there and not in her bag, where it should have been?"

Marissa licked her lips and glanced around. Unlike Milton, she wasn't nearly as calm. I noticed she was rubbing her hands over and over.

"I honestly don't know. Are you insinuating something?"

"Seriously, officer, I'm sorry, deputy," Milton said, stepping forward and interrupting Tucker. "I don't know what you're getting at it. It's true my wife carried an EpiPen, but you don't know if that was hers. There's no label on it I can see. My wife's death was a tragic accident. Nothing more than that. Now, if you can let us grieve in peace, it would be appreciated."

"Us?" I asked, unable to keep quiet. "What do you mean? I thought you didn't have any children."

"Figure of speech," Milton said, but splotches of color were now visible on his neck. "Are we free to go?"

Tucker tilted his head to the side and smiled at Milton, but the effect wasn't a normal grin. No, the deputy resembled a shark.

"Your wife was allergic to shellfish, correct?"

"I believe so. Why?"

"I spoke with the hike's organizer and she claims there was nothing with shellfish in any of the food that was served. But traces were found in your wife's stomach, and in her bloodstream. It's most odd."

"Well, there must have been some cross-contamination," Milton said, shaking his head. "If that's true, I'll be pursuing a wrongful death lawsuit against Wild Peak Expeditions and their food supplier. In fact, I've been speaking to a lawyer friend about this tragedy. My accountant firm has handled his books for years. He's already agreed to represent me. Darlene was taken much too soon, and I can't let my grief cloud my thinking. Someone was responsible, and they need to pay."

Milton looked incredibly pious as he nodded to make his point.

"Would that be the same accountant firm where Miss Whitmore is also employed? The firm where you two have worked there together for the past five years?" Tucker asked.

Silence fell in the lobby. Everything clicked into place. Milton and Marissa weren't complete strangers, brought together by chance, bonded by grief. I looked at Deputy Tucker with new respect. I'd thought he was nothing more than a bumbling jerk, but obviously, Tessa had been right about his law enforcement skills.

"I don't see how our work relationship has anything to do with this," Milton said, raising his chin.

Marissa was silent, but she kept rubbing her hands together. Something tickled my brain, just out of reach. Razzy's fur brushed my leg, and she began pawing at something under the desk.

"So, you're telling me the fact that your wife didn't have her EpiPen in her bag, and your colleague was observed going into a restroom at the trailhead, where an EpiPen was found, is a complete and utter coincidence?" Tucker asked, his voice full of mocking disbelief.

Razzy bumped my shin, and I looked down at her again. She was staring at me so hard I could almost see her thoughts in a little bubble over her head. She pointedly looked at the safe under the desk she was pawing at. Darlene's bag! I bent down, spun the dial on the door, and slid the bag out. My heart rate picked up as a memory came flooding back. I stood and held up the bag, triumphant.

"The bag! I know why she had so much tropomyosin in her system," I said, looking around at everyone before focusing on Marissa. "The bug lotion. I remember you let her use yours, but she didn't give it back. She put it in this bag. But it's not here now. That's what was missing. I knew it!"

Hannah moved closer, her eyes bright as she nodded.

"That's right. I remember. Darlene made a big scene about the chemicals and you," Hannah said, pointing towards Marissa. "You offered her the organic stuff."

"That means nothing," Marissa said, her voice pitched a little higher than normal. "It was just bug lotion. Nothing bad."

"Then where is it?" I asked as I put the bag on the table. "We went through this yesterday and it wasn't there. I know I saw her put it in there."

"Maybe it fell out. You can't prove I took it back."

"No," Hannah said, shaking her head. "You were the one who offered to pick up her things after I dumped the bag out, looking for the EpiPen. You took it back because you knew it would link you to her death. You could've flushed the EpiPen, but you didn't. I bet you kept the lotion as well. You killed Darlene Prescott."

"It wasn't just that, was it?" I asked, walking around the desk. "The brownie. She took it from you and you said nothing. You put something in it, didn't you? You knew she loved brownies and couldn't resist one. Because you, Milton, told her. Between the two of you, that poor woman didn't stand a chance."

"Poor woman?" Marissa screeched, her eyes bulging. "She was a monster! She made Milton's life a living hell. You saw how she was. Demanding, pushy. She was horrible. She got everything she deserved!"

Marissa's chest heaved as Deputy Tucker took a pair of cuffs off his belt and motioned for me to back away.

"Miss Whitmore, you're under arrest for the murder of Darlene Prescott."

Marissa stood, her eyes blank as she slowly lifted her hands up, not resisting as Tucker snapped the metal around her wrists.

"I can't believe it," Milton said, shaking his head. "Marissa, why? Why would you do something like that? Darlene wouldn't have hurt a fly."

Her eyes blazed to life, and she lurched forward, startling the deputy with her sudden movement.

"Don't even think about it. I knew this was a terrible idea. I can't believe I let you talk me into this. We did this together, and you know it!"

Milton stepped back, smoothing his shirt over his expansive middle, and shook his head.

"I'm afraid this woman is quite insane, deputy. I assure you, I want to see her prosecuted to the highest level. To think someone I worked with could be capable of something so horrible. She's obviously unbalanced. I can't believe I never noticed. She must have nursed an obsession with me and thought by killing my dear wife, she would have me. It's just so horrible."

Marissa spit on him, twisting in her cuffs like a madwoman.

"I've got tapes, you loser. That's right. I taped all our conversations. Do think I'm going to go down without a fight? This was all your idea! You're a spineless coward. Darlene was right about you."

She dissolved into sobs that wracked her body, rounding her soft shoulders. I couldn't believe how fast she'd flipped on him. The rest of us stood, waiting to see what would happen next. Tucker turned towards Ben.

"I've got another set of cuffs on my belt. Will you do the honors?"

"Gladly."

Milton took one look at Ben coming towards him and darted for the door, moving faster than I ever would've thought possible. He didn't count on Josh, who was still standing by the exit, observing the whole thing with a white face. Or my boss. Josh stepped in front of Milton, blocking his progress, while Marsburg vaulted over the front desk and blocked Milton from turning back. Josh held the squirming man in place while Ben cuffed his arms behind him.

"That's too tight! It's biting into my wrists," Milton said, mewling in pain. "I'll sue! This is police brutality."

"Well, unfortunately for you, I'm not a cop," Ben said. "He's all yours, Deputy."

The fight went out of Milton Prescott, leaving behind a doughy man, crying his eyes out like a giant toddler, denied a treat. My lip curled on its own as I looked back to Marissa, wondering what on earth had possessed her to kill someone for this man.

"Much obliged. I'll transport these two separately, although part of me wouldn't mind seeing what they'd do to each other if I kept them together. My money's on Miss Whitmore."

He eyed Milton Prescott with distaste before speaking into the radio on his shoulder. I sagged against the front desk. It was over. We'd been right, but it didn't feel good. All I felt was sadness as I looked at Darlene's bag, sitting forlornly next to me.

Hannah let out an audible sigh and joined me, scooping Razzy into her arms. I tickled the cat under her chin.

"Thanks, Razz. If it hadn't been for you, I might not have realized what I was missing. By pawing at the safe, you brought it all back."

She couldn't answer me, not in the crowded lobby, but I'm pretty sure she winked at me. Rudy and Gus crowded around, twining around our legs, as a siren sounded in the distance.

Chapter Eighteen

My body and mind both felt numb after Milton and Marissa were taken away. Deputy Tucker said he'd update us, but I wasn't sure I wanted to know anything else about those two. Eventually, we'd probably be called to testify, but that was the last thing I wanted to think about. Marsburg stood, talking with Ben and Josh, while Wendy, Hannah and I stayed at the desk with the cats.

The doors slid open and Charlie dashed in, her hair standing on end in places. Her eyes darted around the lobby until they found me.

"Oh, thank goodness. I heard the sirens and thought something terrible must have happened. You're okay?"

"I'm fine, Charlie. You wouldn't believe what just happened."

She ran a hand through her hair, trying to work out the tangles and narrowed her eyes.

"What did I miss out on?"

"We caught two murderers," Wendy said, her voice breathless. "It was the craziest thing I've ever seen. Prescott tried to escape, but Ben and Mr. Marsburg saved the day. Oh, and Josh, too."

"Wait, wait, wait. Start over," Charlie said, shaking her head. "From the beginning."

She came over and leaned against the desk while we all took turns with the story. I included how Razzy had tipped me off and Wendy looked at the cat in Hannah's arms, her face beaming.

"They're just so smart. It's almost like they know exactly what's going on. They're extraordinary cats."

I heard Rudy mumble 'almost?' under his breath and couldn't hide my smile. I couldn't shout about their abilities from the rooftops, but I could only hope they knew how much they were appreciated. I bent down to pick him up and cuddle him close, whispering into his fur.

Ben walked over and put his arm around Hannah's waist, pulling her close to his side.

"Well, honey, that settles the case. As much as I'd like to stay, it's about time for us to head back. We've got work tomorrow."

"Shoot. I do, don't I? I've had so much fun up here, I totally forgot about it. There's one more thing we need to do before we go, though."

She gave me a serious look, and I nodded. I'd put this off long enough. It was time to talk to Fig and Oscar about Luna's kits. If Hannah wanted to go with me as moral support, I wasn't about to say no. I nodded and put Rudy down.

"There's something I need to do. I'll see you both at dinner."

Charlie gave me a long look, but nodded. She knew I'd fill her in as soon as I could. Wendy looked a little confused, but soon shrugged and leaned over to give Hannah and Ben a hug.

"It was so nice meeting both of you. I hope you'll come back and visit us sometime."

"We will," she said, without hesitation. "We love it here. Maybe next time we'll have more time to enjoy the resort. I feel like we've been running back and forth since we got here."

Charlie followed Wendy with her own hug and scratched Razzy under the chin.

"I'm glad you were here," she said, her eyes serious as she looked at Hannah. "I know how highly Eden thinks of you and after meeting you both, I can see why. See you soon."

"Take care of each other," Hannah said, smoothing Charlie's rumpled hair. "I feel like we're all family."

Ben went to grab the bags from my office while the rest of us exchanged more hugs and laughed a little. The oppressive gloom, left behind by Milton and Marissa, faded as I realized just how lucky I was to have friends like the ones I had. People with hearts this good didn't grow on trees, and I'd been blessed to have them in my life. Ben stood, hefting two of the bags, and I led them out of the resort, back to my cabin.

As soon as I opened the door, the yowling started and I couldn't help but smile as the three kittens scampered towards us, little tails held high. Ben quickly shut the door to make sure they wouldn't escape.

Luna was curled up in the chair, blinking at us sleepily, but Jasper was sitting bolt upright on the bed, his face creased in concern.

"What's been going on? I heard the sirens."

I plopped down next to him.

"We caught the murderers. I'll tell you all about it later. But there's something we need to do first. It's time," I said, looking over at Luna, who was now paying full attention.

Hannah released the three cats from their bags, and we waited while everyone greeted each other. I couldn't help but notice that Razzy and Luna were getting along better, and it made me smile.

"I'll come with you," Luna said, her voice a little shaky. "I should be there to talk to Fig. But I can't leave the kits alone. They're too young to come with us. I'm not... I'm not ready for them to join the clowder just yet. I don't care what Oscar says. They need another week. Maybe two."

I wondered if Luna had thoughts about staying behind, leaving the clowder life for the comparatively luxurious confines of my cabin.

"I'll stay and watch them," Ben said. "If you don't mind."

Luna looked him over and gave a decisive nod.

"That will be fine. Jasper?"

He got to his feet and stretched.

"I'm coming, too. Just in case."

He didn't elaborate, but I knew what he meant. He was coming to help me convince Fig in case she ended up picking today to be stubborn. In all fairness, she picked every day to be stubborn, but some days were worse than others. I got back up as Hannah checked everyone's harnesses. I spotted Gus giving Ben a look, but in the end, he came with us. We headed out of the cabin, and I could only laugh about what people might think if they caught sight of us, two women with five cats, marching towards the trees.

As we walked, we told Jasper about how we'd figured out who killed Darlene Prescott, and the drama with their arrests. He shook his head and looked at Razzy, pride clear in his golden eyes.

"You're a smart cat. You all are. I'm glad you helped the humans, even though you don't need to."

Razzy looked so pleased I thought she'd burst. Jasper didn't hand out compliments often, but when he did, he meant them. Gus and Rudy looked at the older cat with something close to awe.

"Thank you," Razzy said, dipping her head.

Luna stopped, the tall grass tickling her fur, and spun around. Her distressed eyes met mine as we all came to a halt.

"What is it, Luna?"

"How will I know my little girl is safe? Ever since I've met you, Eden, I've learned that humans can be kind, but they can also be cruel. If not to cats, to each other. I don't know if I'm making the right decision."

I knelt next to the white cat, but it was Jasper who answered her.

"Danger lurks everywhere. Sometimes it hides in the most unexpected places, brought about by someone you thought you knew. But kindness is there too, shining its bright light, beating back the shadows. I lived among humans before, as you know, and I learned many things. Most of all, I learned that there are people out there with good hearts. Eden is one of those people. Hannah and Ben are as well. There are no guarantees in life, Luna. You know this as well as I. But the clowder is no place for a deaf cat. As much as we love your little girl, as much as the clowder would protect and cherish her, it's simply too dangerous."

Luna's head hung down and my heart clenched painfully. I'd learned just how vulnerable the lives of feral cats could be. I turned to Jasper and stroked his grizzled head.

"I was hoping for a better time, a better way to ask this, but Jasper, how would you feel if we adopted the kitten?"

His whiskers curled up in a kitty grin and he nodded.

"I was going to suggest it if you didn't. In the clowder, kits are assigned to the mature adults, who act as mentors. Luna, if you agree, it would be an honor if your kit stayed with us. I promise you to teach her the ways of our clowder. Just as I did when you were young."

Luna looked up, got up, and slowly approached Jasper. She lowered her head in front of him.

"She could have no better teacher. I am honored. And Eden, she could have no better human. Would you... Would you bring her to me sometimes? Or maybe I could visit..."

A smile broke over my face, and it felt as though the clouds had cleared.

"Of course. Any time. I'll do my best to keep her safe and she'll always know she's loved."

Hannah sniffed, and I turned to see tears running down her cheeks. She backhanded them away as Razzy crowded close to her.

"Sorry, it's just so touching."

I cleared my throat as tears threatened to clog it. We hadn't even asked Fig yet, and I was already emotional. I stood and scrubbed at my face with my hands. Luna bumped Jasper and ran her head along his flank before standing and marching towards the trees.

"She'll be fine with it, you know," Jasper said. "Fig wants what is best for all the cats in her care. And this is what's best for Luna and her kit."

I nodded as we entered the forest. Fig always had someone watching, and I knew she'd join us in minutes as soon as our presence was noted. Razzy, Rudy, and Gus stayed a respectful distance away from the rock where the brown cat always sat and we settled in to wait.

A familiar tortoiseshell cat walked through the trees and I smiled, waving at her.

"Willow! It's good to see you. Is Fig around?"

"She's on her way. I was hunting with Ollie and let him know everyone was here. What's going on? This isn't the usual time of day you visit us."

She greeted the other cats, paying special attention to Rudy. He sat, his spine straight, whiskers bristled as she looked back at him with a mischievous light in her pretty eyes. Razzy and Gus exchanged a look over his head, and I overheard Gus's whispered comment.

"Callie might have some competition."

I thought about the irrepressible calico cat who lived with our friend Anastasia and smiled. Her favorite pastime was flinging herself at anyone who visited Anastasia's shop, and she had more energy than two cats combined. She'd belonged to the clowder once as well.

A slight rustling sound heralded Fig's arrival, and she leapt nimbly on top of the rock, surveying all of us.

"Luna. It's good to see you back in the forest. Where are your kits? It's past the time for them to join their family."

The white cat sat below the rock and glanced at Jasper before speaking.

"I know. They will come home soon. Maybe next week. The kits are the reason we have come."

Fig tilted her head to the side and looked at Jasper. Her tail flicked, and he moved to join her as she shifted to the side to allow him space. Even though she led the clowder now, her respect for Jasper was obvious.

"I see. Our visiting friends are still among us. The last time they stayed, they took a kit with them. How is young Callie?"

Razzy glanced at Rudy, who was in deep discussion with Willow, before answering.

"She is thriving, Fig. She is a cat to be proud of. Her heart is true."

"Hmmm. That is gratifying to hear. The hunting parties are

returning and I must get back to our dens. Luna, you said the kits are the reason you are here, but they are not with you. I can guess why you are here."

One of the many things I respected about Fig was her ability to be direct and not dance around a subject, however painful it might be.

"There is no need to guess, Fig," Luna said, her voice clear. "The two tom kits will come home soon, but the girl... She will stay with Eden and Jasper. Even though she is a brave and fierce kit, she cannot hear."

Fig's yellow eyes blazed and her fur fluffed.

"You are certain?"

"We are," Rudy said, leaving Willow and marching towards the rock, tail held high. "I tested her several times. She is special. The best place for her is with Eden."

Fig softened as she looked at the earnest young cat in front of her.

"That took courage. You have grown from the young tom you were when we last met. Jasper, what is your opinion?"

"Rudy is right. Luna and I noticed it as well, but we thought perhaps she was developing slower than her brothers. Eden and I will take responsibility for her, guide her, teach her, and keep her safe."

"Have you asked Oscar?"

Luna bristled, and the grass at her feet rustled as she dug her claws into the earth.

"I have not. I am their mother. It is my decision."

Fig hopped down from the rock and walked to Luna, circling her before coming to a seat in front of the white cat.

"Motherhood has agreed with you. I see you have grown a spine. Very well, I accept. She will remain with the human, outside of the clowder, but loved not less for it."

My shoulders slowly relaxed and I let out a long breath. Fig must have heard as she gave me a quick glance and flicked her tail.

"Love her well, Eden. The world is a harsh place for special cats."

"I know. I will."

She nodded towards Jasper and flicked her tail again, prompting Willow to move forward. She shyly touched noses with Rudy before melting back into the trees, right behind Fig. Razzy stretched, rolling her back like a wave.

"That went well. I suppose we have to go home now?"

Hannah nodded and gathered up their leashes.

"We do, baby girl."

We started the long walk back to the cabin, but this time, the mood was joyous. I still wasn't certain how Oscar was going to feel about it, but it was clear Luna could handle it. The white cat seemed lighter, more settled now that we had a plan for her kit. Once again, she walked next to Razzy. It appeared the two queens had solved their differences.

Rudy and Gus flanked them while Jasper hung back with me. I knew he was tired and scooped him up to nuzzle his forehead.

"Sorry, I needed a hug," I said.

He looked into my eyes and his expression told me he understood my ulterior motive and didn't mind. He settled into my arms, his raspy purr reverberating through my chest.

"Hugs are very important."

Silence enveloped us as we approached the cabin, but it wasn't heavy. It was as light as a feather, wrapping us in contentment. I opened the door and stepped aside so everyone could enter before us. Hannah's delighted laugh echoed through the small room and I poked my head around to see Ben, lying on the floor, draped with sleeping kittens.

"I didn't dare move and wake them," he said, murmuring as they stirred. "How did it go?"

"Fine," Luna said as the kitten's sleepy meows sounded. "Everything is going to be just fine."

They scrambled to their mother, freeing Ben, who stood with a grin and wrapped Hannah in a hug.

"All set to go home?"

"Yes, but I'm going to miss it here," Hannah said, glancing at me as I put Jasper on the bed. "Even with all that's happened, it's been so nice hanging out with you, Eden. And all the cats."

Razzy watched as the kittens played around their mother and tilted her head to the side, her eyes soft.

"When will you name them?"

Luna met her eyes.

"Soon. I will let Oscar name the boys. That should soften the blow a little. But I want to name this one," she said, bumping the girl with her nose. "She needs something special."

"Her mother is named for the moon," Razzy said, her voice quiet. "And I think this one is going to be a star."

Luna blinked, surprised, and let out a low purr.

"That's it. I will name her Star. It's perfect."

Rudy let out a sound that was a mix of a purr and a chirp and, once again, tears threatened to spill down my cheeks. The small white kitten was definitely going to be special, and now she had a name that would let the world know how brightly she would shine.

"I love it."

The cats said their goodbyes as Hannah and Ben trailed out of the cabin, clearly not wanting to leave. I'd grown so used to having them close it was going to be hard to see them drive away.

"I'm so happy you're here," Hannah said, wiping her cheeks as Ben opened the door. "But I wish you were closer. We'll try to come visit more often."

"And maybe you can come visit us in Golden Hills," Ben said, slinging a bag over his shoulder. "We'd love that. You can bring as many cats that will fit in your car."

I chuckled, imagining transporting them to Hannah's town. It would definitely be an experience. I knelt as Hannah brought out the carrying bags. I was going to miss these dear cats.

"I had a lot of fun," Rudy said, leaning against me. "Take care of everyone. Tell Willow I'll maybe see her again. Next time."

"I will," I said, picking him up so I could give him a kiss on the head. "Thank you for helping Star."

Razzy and Gus waited at my feet while Rudy got into his bag and turned around so Hannah could zip him in.

"Gus, you take care of everyone, okay? And I know they'll take care of you."

His tufted ears tickled my cheek as I brought him in for a hug.

"You too, Eden. We'll see you again."

Once he was loaded up, I turned to Razzy. Not so long ago, she'd helped me when I was in the depths of despair. They all had. I owed them all so much, but I didn't know how I could ever repay them. She blinked her beautiful eyes as I held her in my arms.

"I don't know where I'd be if it wasn't for you," I said, whispering into her fur. "Thank you."

She surprised me with a raspy lick on the cheek that made me giggle.

"Cheer up, Eden. It won't be long before we see each other again. We can FaceTime, too. I want to see how Star is doing. And Jasper, of course."

This time, the tears refused to stay put, and streamed down my face as I helped get everyone loaded into the car. Once the last bag was stowed, Hannah turned and pulled me into a fierce hug, holding me tightly.

"I'll miss you. Keep in touch, okay? And don't be afraid to leap. When the time is right, you'll know."

She pulled away as Ben walked over and wrapped her in a one-armed hug, placing a kiss on the top of her head. She leaned into him for a moment before getting in the Blazer and buckling her seat belt. Ben gave me a quick hug before hustling over to the driver's side and getting in.

Hannah rolled down the window and waved as they pulled away, and I could hear the chorus from the cats, wishing me well. I wrapped my arms around my waist and headed back to my cabin. The sun was setting, painting the sky in hues of pink and purple.

I paused at the door to my cabin, appreciating the surrounding beauty. This weekend hadn't gone the way I'd planned, but I was lucky enough to be surrounded by great friends, both human and feline. I knew no matter what direction my life took, I could always count on them. Summer was just beginning and something told me there were plenty more adventures ahead.

Don't Miss A Taste of Trouble!

Summer has come to Valewood, and the temperatures aren't the only thing that's heating up. Tensions are running high as the Valewood Resort hosts a food truck festival, and Eden Brooks is determined that this time, everything is going to go smoothly.

Unfortunately, the competitors didn't get the memo, and their rivalry threatens to impact everyone at the resort. It's going to take everything the Valewood crew's got to keep the peace and keep their guests happy.

As if she didn't have enough on her plate, Eden's family arrives unexpectedly, throwing her predictable routine into chaos.

Just when she didn't think things could get any worse, something terrible happens, and Eden's thrown into the deep end once again. She's going to need the help of all of her friends, human and feline, to get to the bottom of this one.

Already Missing Finn and Briar? (And Tessa, too)

Look for a new series starting in early 2025!

Have you read The Razzy Cat Cozy Mystery Series?

The Body in the Park
A Razzy Cat Cozy Mystery

"I'm a cat lover and read many cat mysteries. Courtney McFarlin's Razzy Cat Cozy Mystery Series is my favorite."

She's found an unlikely consultant to help solve the crime. But this speaking pet might just prove purr-fect...

Hannah Murphy yearns for a real news story. But after a strange migraine results in an unexpected ability to talk to her cat, she must keep the kitty-communication skills a secret if she wants to advance from fluff pieces to covering felonies. And when she literally trips over a slain body, she's shocked her feline companion is the best partner to crack the case.

Convinced she's finally got her big break, Hannah quickly runs afoul of a handsome detective and his poor opinion of interfering reporters. And when she discovers the victim's penchant for embezzlement and fraud, she may need more than a furry friend and a cantankerous cop to avoid ending up in the obits.

Can Hannah catch a killer before her career and her life are dead and buried?

The Body in the Park is the delightful first book in the Razzy Cat cozy mystery series. If you like clever sleuths, light banter, and talking animals, then you'll love Courtney McFarlin's hilarious whodunit.

More reader comments: "The Razzy Cat series is a joy to read! I have read the first three, and just bought the fourth. These books are well written, engaging stories. I love the positive and supportive relationships depicted amongst the main characters and the cats. That is so refreshing to read. I look forward to more books in this series. I will also be reading some this author's other works. Well done, and keep writing!" - Ingrid

Buy *The Body in the Park* for the long arm of the paw today!

Books By Courtney McFarlin

A Razzy Cat Cozy Mystery Series

The Body in the Park

The Trouble at City Hall

The Crime at the Lake

The Thief in the Night

The Mess at the Banquet

The Girl Who Disappeared

Tails by the Fireplace

The Love That Was Lost

The Problem at the Picnic

The Chaos at the Campground

The Crisis at the Wedding

The Murder on the Mountain

The Reunion on the Farm

The Mishap at the Meeting

The Bones on the Trail

The Dispute at the Fair

The Commotion at the Race - Winter 2024

A Soul Seeker Cozy Mystery

The Apparition in the Attic

The Banshee in the Bathroom

The Creature in the Cabin

The ABCs of Seeing Ghosts

The Demon in the Den

The Ether in the Entryway

The Fright in the Family Room

The Ghoul in the Garage

The Haunting in the Hallway

The Imp at the Ice Rink

The Jinn in the Joists

The Kelpie in the Kennel

The Lady in the Library

The Clowder Cats Cozy Mystery Series

Resorting to Murder

A Slippery Slope

A Mountain of Mischief

Pushing Up Daisies

A Taste of Trouble - Coming Spring of 2025!

Millie the Miracle Cat Cozy Mystery Series

A New Beginning

Stacked Against Us

Volumes of Lies - End of 2024

A Siren's Song Paranormal Cozy Mystery Series

The Wrong Note

A Major Case

The Missing Beat - Early 2025

Escape from Reality Cozy Mystery Series

Escape from Danger

Escape from the Past

Escape from Hiding

A Note From Courtney

Thank you for taking the time to read this novel. If you enjoyed the book, please take a few minutes to leave a review. As an independent author, I appreciate the help!

If you'd like to be first in line to hear about new books as they are released, don't forget to sign up for my newsletter. Click here to sign up! https://bit.ly/2H8BSef

A Little About Me

Courtney McFarlin currently lives in the Black Hills of South Dakota with her fiancé and their two cats.

Find out more about her books at:
www.booksbycourtney.com

Follow Courtney on Social Media:

https://twitter.com/booksbycourtney

https://www.instagram.com/courtneymcfarlin/

https://www.facebook.com/booksbycourtneym

Made in the USA
Monee, IL
13 November 2024